"Li
go

"Why are you so upset? It's my problem, not yours."

He felt as though she'd punched him, hard. "Marise is my daughter, too—don't you think it's about time you admitted that? I'm going to meet her, Lia, whether you want me to or not."

"We'll see," Lia said, her jaw a stubborn jut.

"Don't try and stop me," he said very quietly. "You'll regret it if you do."

"Are you threatening me?"

"I'm telling you the truth."

Her nostrils flared. "So what am I supposed to do?"

"Marry me," Seth said.

The words echoed in his head. What in hell had possessed him to say them? He didn't want to marry Lia. He didn't want to marry anyone.

Sandra Field

HIS ONE-NIGHT MISTRESS

FOR Love OR MONEY

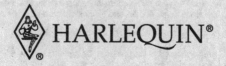

HARLEQUIN®

TORONTO • NEW YORK • LONDON
AMSTERDAM • PARIS • SYDNEY • HAMBURG
STOCKHOLM • ATHENS • TOKYO • MILAN • MADRID
PRAGUE • WARSAW • BUDAPEST • AUCKLAND

ISBN 0-373-12494-5

HIS ONE-NIGHT MISTRESS

First North American Publication 2005.

Copyright © 2005 by Sandra Field.

This edition published by arrangement with Harlequin Books S.A.

www.eHarlequin.com

Printed in U.S.A.

CHAPTER ONE

GLITTERING. Dazzling. *Magnifique!*

Lia d'Angeli edged toward the wall in the vast foyer of the hotel, whose floor-to-ceiling, gilt-scrolled mirrors reflected what could have been a scene from one of Louis XIV's revels. Her fingers tightened around her invitation with its elegant gold script, an invitation given her just yesterday by her Parisian friend Mathieu. "A masked ball," he'd said with his charming, lop-sided grin. "I can't go, *malheureusement.* Take some handsome young man, Lia, eat, drink and dance your heart out." His grin took on a satyr's edge. "You could try ending up in his bed——you're far too beautiful to have the reputation of a nun, *chérie.*"

Mathieu's endearment Lia took with a grain of salt; he was known for romantic dalliance in every district of Paris. But his advice——at least some of it—she fully intended to take. Eat, drink and dance. Yes, she'd do all three with pleasure. But she had come to the ball alone, and she intended to leave it alone.

Alone and anonymous, she thought with a sigh of pure pleasure. Her fame was new, and not altogether pleasant. But this evening she wasn't Lia d'Angeli, the brilliant young violinist who'd burst on the international scene by winning two prestigious competitions within six months of each other. No, she thought, glancing sideways at herself in the nearest mirror and feeling her lips curve in a smile. She was a butterfly instead, flirtatious and enigmatic, fluttering from partner to partner with no intention of being pinned down by any one of them.

Her costume consisted of a shiny turquoise bodysuit that faithfully outlined her breasts, hips, gently incurving waist and long, slender legs. Jeweled turquoise sandals were on her feet. Flaring between arm and thigh were her wings, folds of delicate chiffon, turquoise and green. But it was her mask that made the costume. Like a helmet, it covered her high cheekbones, revealing only the darkness of her eyes, and hiding her tumble of black hair in a glimmer of sequins and exquisite peacock feathers. She'd carefully smoothed turquoise makeup over her cheeks, her chin and her throat; her lips were a luminous gold.

An outrageous costume, she thought with great satisfaction. A costume that freed her to be anyone she wanted to be.

No one here knew her. She planned to take full advantage of that, dance her heart out and leave by midnight. Just like Cinderella.

Her eyes ranged the crowd. Marie Antoinette, the Hunchback of Notre-Dame, a cardinal worthy of an El Greco portrait, a sexy dancer from the Moulin Rouge. All masked. All strangers to each other. And perhaps to themselves, she thought with a tiny shiver of her nerves.

She shook off her sudden unease, making her way to the doorman and presenting her numbered invitation. A uniformed official was whispering something in his ear; the doorman waved her into the ballroom impatiently, scarcely glancing at the calligraphy on the card as he added it to the stack beside him. Lia slipped past him quickly; she'd worried a little that there might be some objection to her having Mathieu's invitation rather than one in her own name. A good omen, she thought lightheartedly, and tucked herself around the corner out of his sight.

The ballroom was alive with the lilt of an old-fashioned waltz, although by the look of the sound equipment the music wouldn't be that sedate all evening. More mirrors adorned the sapphire-blue walls, while sparkling gold chandeliers were suspended from a ceiling painted with more chubby cherubs than there were springtime lovers in Paris. Against the far wall long tables with immaculate white cloths held a feast that even King Louis wouldn't have scorned. White-jacketed waiters circulated among the crowd, holding aloft silver trays of wine and champagne.

And then she saw him.

Like herself, the man was standing with his back to the wall, surveying the crowd. A highwayman, cloaked and booted, a black mask making slits of his eyes, a black hat with a sweeping brim shadowing his features.

No costume in the world could have hidden his height, the breadth of his shoulders or his aura of power, of command, of complete and utter self-control. An aura he clearly took for granted.

A man who took what he wanted. A highwayman, indeed.

He, like her, was alone.

As another of those chills traced the length of Lia's spine, his gaze came to rest on her. Even across the width of the huge ballroom, she felt his sudden, searing focus; his body stilled, like a bandit's when he sights his victim.

She couldn't have moved to save her soul.

The butterfly pinned to the wall, she thought crazily, her heart racing against her rib cage. She'd been frightened many times in her life; it was part of the striving for excellence that had driven her for as long as she could remember. But pre-concert nerves, for all their terrors, were at least backed by the sure knowledge of her own technical accomplishments, and by the inner certainty that, once again, she could over-come those nerves.

This terror was different. She felt stripped, laid bare, ex-posed. All because a stranger had chanced to look at her. A man she'd never seen before——of that she was sure——and need never see again.

Ridiculous, she thought, gathering every vestige of her courage to fight an assault unlike any she'd ever known.

Assault? The man hadn't even touched her.

In a flare of defiance Lia gestured to the nearest waiter, took a glass of red wine from his tray and, with a mocking salute to the man across the room, raised the glass in a toast.

He swept off his hat, revealing a crop of untidy, sun-streaked blond hair, and bowed to her from the waist, a courtly gesture that brought an involuntary smile to her lips. Then he straightened and started toward her across the wide expanse of floor.

In total panic she heard a male voice say in clumsily ac-cented French, *"Voulez-vous danser avec moi, madame?"*

A British soldier from the Napoleonic wars had inserted himself between her and the highwayman. Quickly Lia put her wine down on the nearest table and said, in English, "Thank you, yes."

"Cool—you speak English," the soldier said, put his arm around her and with a certain flair eased her among the other dancers. He waltzed with a competence for which she was grateful, and didn't seem to require much from her in the way of conversation, for which she was more than grateful. From the corner of her eye, she watched the highwayman be ac-costed by a group of curvaceous chorus girls, then extract him-self with a remark that left them all giggling. She said breathlessly, "I'd love to get a closer look at the orchestra——can we go that way?"

The soldier obediently whisked her to the opposite end of

the room. The waltz ended, followed by a rhumba. A clown with a garish red slash of mouth cut in; automatically Lia followed the rhythm, her diaphanous wings fluttering as she raised and lowered her arms. The clown was superseded by a dignified gentleman who could have emerged from the pages of a Jane Austen novel.

As the two-step came to its predictable close, another partner loomed behind the elderly gentleman. The highwayman, his black cloak swirling. Lia's nerves tightened to an almost intolerable pitch, even though from the first moment she'd seen him she'd known this meeting was inevitable. "My turn, I believe," he said pleasantly, yet with an edge of steel underlying a voice as smooth as brandy.

Lia smiled at her partner, thanked him and turned to face her opponent. For opponent he was; of that she was in no doubt.

She could have refused to speak to him. But pride had always been one of her besetting sins, and besides, weren't challenges meant to be met?

Before she could even open her mouth, he said with that same steel edge, "You've had your fun. Now it's my turn."

She'd see about that. Raising her chin, Lia said with rather overdone politeness, "It's very warm in here, isn't it? I'd love a glass of champagne."

"What's your name?"

"Subtlety certainly isn't yours."

"I don't believe in wasting time."

"Mine or yours?" she demanded.

"Mine."

"Then perhaps you should find yourself another partner."

"Oh, I don't think so," he said.

"So tell me *your* name," she said, fully expecting him to refuse.

"Seth Talbot. From Manhattan. You're American as well."

Her home base was a tiny apartment in Greenwich Village.

She said coolly, "I was born in Switzerland, Mr. Talbot," and with equal aplomb gestured to the nearest waiter, who presented her with a crystal flute of champagne. She raised it to her lips, feeling the bubbles tickle her nostrils.

"So you take what you want," Seth Talbot said softly.

"Is there any other way?"

"Not in my world. I'm glad we understand each other."

"You can't possibly understand me—because you don't know what I want," she retorted.

"From the first moment we caught sight of each other, we've wanted the same thing."

Back off, Lia. Be sensible. End this before it begins. "Since I'm no mind reader," she snapped, "why don't you tell me what that is?"

He wrapped fingers as unyielding as handcuffs around her wrist. Long, lean fingers, she saw, ringless, with well-kept nails and a dusting of blond hair where his shirt ended in a tight cuff. She said evenly, "Let go."

With almost insulting abruptness he dropped her wrist. The music had started again. "We're in the way," he said, draped an arm around Lia's shoulders and drew her off the dance floor.

His cloak had enveloped her in its dark folds; his arm was heavy, its weight as intimate as a caress. She could have protested. Screamed, even. In a room full of people there was no way he could do anything to her without her consent.

Had she ever felt like this in her life? It was as though he'd mesmerized her. Her heart was beating in slow heavy strokes, and the warmth from his arm had spread throughout her limbs. From a long way away, Lia watched him toss his hat on a table. He took her free hand in his and raised it to his lips, caressing her knuckles. Then he turned her hand over and kissed her palm with lingering sensuality.

His hair was thick and silky clean. All she wanted to do

was drop her champagne glass on the floor and drag her fingers through those untidy, gold-tipped waves, exploring the tautness of his scalp, cupping her hand to his nape. With a physical effort that felt enormous, Lia gripped the stem of her glass, holding onto it as if it were all that was keeping her sane.

His mouth was still drifting over her palm. Her eyes closed as sensation swept through her in waves of pleasure. Deep inside her, desire sprang to life in a tumultuous, imperative ache; for a few moments that were outside of time Lia gave herself over to it, her body as boneless as a butterfly's. She was spreading her wings to the sun, she thought dizzily. Drawing in its heat, laved by its golden rays. Fully alive, as surely she was meant to be.

Come off it, Lia. Say it like it is. You're allowing yourself to be seduced by a man who lives in the same city as you.

She snatched her hand back, champagne sloshing over her dainty shoes, and said raggedly, "You've got to stop!"

He lifted his head, although he was still clasping her fingers. "You don't want me to stop——tell the truth."

"I don't know the first thing about you, yet you're——"

"We've skipped the preliminaries, that's all," he said hoarsely. "Gone for the essentials."

With a jolt of her heart she heard that roughness in his voice, and saw how the pulse at the base of his throat was pounding against his skin. "You feel it, too," she whispered.

"I felt it the first moment I saw you across the room."

Hadn't she known that? Wasn't that why she'd run for the dance floor with the nearest available man, and stayed there as long as she could? She said faintly, "A highwayman's a thief, Mr. Talbot."

"A butterfly's sole purpose is to mate."

Her breath hissed between her teeth. "A thief takes what he wants regardless of the consequences."

"If you're willing to be taken, I can scarcely be called a thief."

"Oh, stop it," Lia said peevishly, "you're turning me around in circles."

"Good," he said, and suddenly smiled at her.

It was a smile that crackled with pure male energy. Steeling herself against it, Lia clipped off her words with cold precision. "I'm not looking for a mate. A costume's just that——a costume. Not a statement about my character."

He looked her up and down, taking his time, his gaze scorching her flesh almost as though she was naked. "Yet you look highly provocative."

Two could play that game, Lia thought in a flare of temper. She glanced downward. His soft leather boots clung to his calves and were cuffed at the knees; his thighs were black-clad, strongly muscled against the taut fabric. Her eyes traveled upward, past his elegant white shirt with its laced neckline over a slash of tanned skin, to the wide shoulders under his cloak. A wave of primitive hunger attacked her, shocking her with its intensity. Had she ever felt this way in her life?

No, she hadn't. Ever. She said with admirable coolness, "Let's face it, you didn't choose to dress up as a clown with ears like jugs and white paint all over your face—like the one I danced with a few minutes ago. Your costume's sexy, too. So what?"

"You're finally admitting you find me sexy——we're making progress."

"Don't be coy," she said, exasperated. "I've got eyes in my head and any woman worthy of the name would find you sexy."

His voice roughened. "This is all very amusing and it's nowhere near the truth. There's something going on between us that's never happened to me before——not like this. Not once in my life have I seen a woman across a crowded room and known in my blood and my bones that I had to have her. You've got to trust me on that—I swear it's true."

The crazy thing was that she believed him instantly. "This kind of thing's never happened to me, either," she said shakily.

With a gentleness that disarmed her, he stroked her cheek with one finger. "Thanks——for being so honest."

Longing simply to rest her forehead against his shoulder and be held by him, Lia said as steadily as she could, "Then let me continue to be honest. I don't make a habit of getting into bed with strangers."

"Neither do I. So why don't we begin with you telling me your name?"

She'd come here to be anonymous; and from some deep instinct, she intended to remain so. Tossing her head, she said, "I can give you a false name. Or no name at all. Your choice."

He took her glass from her hand and thunked it on the table beside his hat. "Why are you being so mysterious?"

"It suits my purposes."

His eyes narrowed. "Are you someone I should know?"

He didn't look the type of man to sit in a concert hall listening to Beethoven; he'd be more at home in a smoky jazz bar. "I doubt it," she said.

"If we go to bed tonight——and that's what we're talking about——I have to know who you are."

He was right, she thought in horror, she *was* considering going to bed with him. Was she clean out of her mind? "If you insist on knowing my name," she said, "then it's no dice."

"Are you in trouble with the law?"

"No!"

"If you're neither famous nor on the lam, you could have given me a false name and I'd never know the difference."

"I dislike lying."

"You like winning."

She laughed, a warm throaty chuckle. "Well, of course. Is there anything wrong with that?"

"I like winning, too."

"Then——as far as my name's concerned—it'll be good for you to have a new experience. We should all expand our horizons occasionally, Mr. Talbot."

"The name's Seth," he said tersely. "And even though you may disbelieve this, I've had more than enough experience of losing in my life."

Her smile faded; once again she believed him instantly and wholeheartedly. "For that, I'm sorry," she said.

"You are, aren't you?" he said in an odd voice. "You're beginning to intrigue me——is this about more than lust?"

Again panic flared in her chest. She said obliquely, "If a highwayman even noticed anything as ephemeral as a butterfly, he'd crush it underfoot."

"How about my version? He sees it as something so beautiful that he simply wants to enjoy it."

"But then he has to let it fly away," Lia said, and heard in her own voice something of the steel she'd earlier heard in his.

For a moment he was silent, his eyes trained on her face. Then, with a suddenness that startled her, he ripped his mask off and flung it on the floor. His eyes were deep set, a startlingly deep green, flecked with amber. His cheekbones were imperative, and for the first time she saw the full strength of a face that was both too rugged to be truly handsome, and too strongly carved to be anything but formidable. She swallowed hard and said the first thing that came into her head. "I must be mad to be even contemplating going anywhere near a bed with you…and I'm stone cold sober, so I can't blame it on the champagne."

"It's nothing to do with champagne," he said softly. "Take off your mask."

"No," she said. "If we go to bed together, you have to promise not to touch my mask. You'll never know who I am——that's the way I want it and that's the way it's going to play. If you don't agree to my conditions, then I'm walking out of here right now, and if you try to stop me I'll scream the place down."

"So the battle lines are drawn…I could change your mind, you know."

"But you won't try. Not if you respect me as you should."

Incredibly he began to laugh, throwing his head back so the muscles in his throat stood out like cords. Then he looked straight at her. "I have the feeling my life's been entirely too dull and predictable for the last many years. Both in bed and out. I'll tell you one thing——you're not dull, and not the slightest bit predictable."

Wasn't that one of the things the critics always said of her? Lia d'Angeli never plays it safe. Never takes the well-worn path. Risks everything to find the heart and soul of the music.

Nine times out of ten, the risks paid off. But would that be true of tonight? With this man? Or would tonight be the tenth concert, the one the critics pounced on with glee?

She had no way of knowing.

CHAPTER TWO

THE band had struck up a tango, a dance that was a battle of the sexes. Meeting Seth's eyes full on, Lia said, "You don't look like someone who'd live a dull life."

With an underlying bitterness Seth said, "Appearances can be deceptive, pretty butterfly."

So he had indeed known unhappiness, this tall stranger in the black cloak. Somehow that strengthened a decision that was already made. Standing tall, Lia said, "Do you agree to my conditions, Seth Talbot? I don't tell you my name, and my mask stays in place."

He stepped closer, took her face between his palms and bent his head to kiss her. It was all there in that one kiss: the compulsion toward each other, the fierce hunger, the dissolving of all her boundaries. His mouth was sure, the slide of his tongue engulfing her in need; his teeth grazed her lips like the flick of fire. Without hesitation Lia met him thrust for thrust, depth to depth, flame wrapped around flame.

Very slowly, he drew back. The green of his eyes had darkened, like a forest falling under the shadows of sundown. His heightened breathing wafted her cheeks as he said unsteadily, "I'd agree to anything to get you in my bed. I don't like your conditions—I don't like them at all. But I agree to them, and I promise I won't go against them."

She let out her pent-up breath in a tiny sigh. With the faintest of smiles she said, "Well. We can stay here, dance, eat, drink and make small talk. Or we can do what we both want to do——go somewhere where we can be alone."

"I like your style," Seth said.

"Life's short," Lia replied, feeling her heart racket in her chest, "and I believe in living on the edge." She gave a sudden rich chuckle. "A cocoon would never be my choice."

He said abruptly, "I'm booked into a suite in this hotel. We'll go there."

Her lashes flickered. A suite here would cost more than she earned in a month. So he was rich, this man from Manhattan. She said lightly, "I've often wondered what it would be like to stay here. Now I'm going to find out."

"So you're not one of the rich socialites who hangs around Paris at this time of year, waiting until she can open her villa on the Riviera?"

The image amused her. "I work exceedingly hard for my money," she said incautiously, "and hanging around wouldn't suit me at all."

"Just how do you earn this money?" he flashed.

She lifted one finger, tracing the sensuous line of his lower lip, and with a tiny flare of power felt his jaw tighten. "I don't think we're really interested in a discussion of our respective occupations," she said. "I earn my living legally, I'm ferociously ambitious, and I guarantee in ten years' time you will have heard of me. And that's all you're getting out of me. Unless—" she smiled at him artlessly "—you've changed your mind about seducing me?"

"I very rarely meet my match," Seth said. "Most particularly in a woman. No, I haven't changed my mind." With ruthless speed he plunged to find her lips, searing them in a kiss as incendiary as it was brief. Raising his head, he said with a calmness belied by the sparks of fire in his eyes, "Shall we go?"

As he offered his arm, Lia rested her hand on it, the frail colors of one wing dulled by the dense black of his cloak. Another frisson of terror flicked along her nerves. Keeping her head up, she stayed close to him as he threaded his way through the masked revelers; and knew in her heart that this was the biggest risk she'd ever taken. The violin was her home territory, known, loved with a passion and, at times, hated with equal passion. But in affairs of the heart, she was a novice.

Unlike, she was sure, Seth Talbot.

They walked past the doorman, who was absorbed in sorting the piles of invitations. The elevator was made of such highly polished brass that she could see her outline in the walls, a shimmer of turquoise. The scarlet-uniformed attendant pushed the button without Seth saying a word: so he was well-known here, she thought, her nerves tightening another notch.

The elevator took them to the top floor. The brass doors smoothly closed behind them. Clasping her by the hand, Seth led the way along a high-ceilinged hallway to a pair of tall cream-colored doors scrolled in gilt, and swung them open, gesturing for her to enter. But her limbs refused to obey her. Frozen to the spot, she croaked, "I don't know the first thing about you."

"You know what's between us——what more do you want?"

Her nostrils flared. "You're six inches taller than I am, you probably weigh seventy pounds more, and if you're not a black-belt in karate, it wouldn't take much for you to become one."

He let out his breath in a small sigh. "I've never in my life crushed a butterfly, and I'm not about to start with you."

"I'm supposed to believe you? Just like that?"

"I don't know what the hell's going on between us," he rasped, "but it sure isn't casual, that much I do know. We're going to strip each other naked, little butterfly, in more ways than the obvious one. So this is about trust as much as it's about seduction—I thought you'd already figured that out."

"I hadn't," she said, her eyes smoldering behind her mask. "Trust's a very big word."

He added edgily, "I don't force myself on women, that's not to my taste. Plus there's at least one telephone in every room, and all you have to do is pick up the nearest one for an immediate connection to the front desk. You're safer here than you'd be anywhere else in Paris, believe me."

She was damned if she was going to apologize for her attack of nerves. Walk onto the stage, Lia, she thought wildly, and stalked past him into his suite.

It took her breath away. Her eyes ranged from one end of the room to the other, tarrying on the delicate gold chandeliers, the luxurious embroidered brocades and tasseled velvets. The spacious parquet floor was spread with antique hand-woven carpets. "There's even a balcony," she breathed.

"With a wonderful view of the Eiffel Tower," Seth said solemnly. "Would you like to see it?"

All her doubts dropped away. She turned to face him. "Later. Maybe." Then she stood on tiptoes and kissed him with an ardor all the more touching for its lack of expertise.

His eyes narrowed. Taking her face in his hands, he said with careful restraint, "Tell me one thing—you're not a virgin, are you?"

Her head reared back; it never occurred to her to lie. "No, of course not. But I've only been with one man, and that was three years ago. It wasn't about lust on my part, it was about curiosity—and perhaps that's why it didn't move me, body or soul. Serves me right, I suppose."

"I see," said Seth. "Then we'll have to make up for lost time, won't we?" He bent his head, finding her mouth and teasing it open, his tongue dancing along her lips.

She gave a tiny purr of pleasure, molding her body to his, giving herself over to the unknown and the new with the daring that was so characteristic of her. As she thrust her hands beneath his cloak, wrapping them around the taut curves of his rib cage, he dragged her closer; her breasts were crushed to his chest, his arousal so fierce and imperative that she felt a thrill of sheer, feminine power.

His kiss deepened, demanding all she could give. With another thrill of power, Lia knew she wanted to give him everything that was in her, all the passionate hunger for life that had driven her for as long as she could remember. His tongue was hot and slick, his body hard and utterly masculine; reveling in a host of sensations, she dug her fingers in his scalp, pulling his head lower, her knees buckling as wave after wave of desire surged through her belly and throbbed between her thighs.

He muttered between kisses that imprinted her cheeks, her chin, her throat, "We should go slow…it's been a long time for you and I want to give you—"

Her answer was to pull at his shirt, loosening it from his trousers. "Don't fight what's between us," she begged. "I want you now, Seth. Now."

Swiftly he threw his cloak to the floor and hauled his shirt over his head. Lia's breath caught in her throat. "You're so beautiful," she choked, and briefly laid her cheek against his chest. His heart was pounding. His skin smelled cleanly of soap and of the essence of this man who was both a stranger and yet utterly known to her.

He said with that thread of laughter already so familiar to her, "How do I get you out of your costume? You could be sewn into it for all I know."

She turned deliberately in his arms. "There's a zipper down the back," she said, and bowed her head.

His mouth traced the softness of her nape, savoring every inch, sending shudders of longing through her frame. Then he caught the zipper and with a single tug bared the long line of her spine. She turned again, her eyes glittering, eased her arms from the tight sleeves and let her costume fall to her waist.

"God, you're lovely," he breathed, his heated gaze causing her nipples to harden involuntarily. He cupped her breasts, stroking the ivory curves of flesh, then dropped his head to suckle her.

She cried out in instinctive response, her body arching toward him, her eyes closed in ecstasy; and all the while his hands, those wonderfully sensitive hands, were tracing the taut curve of her belly and the delicate arc of her ribs. Her breathing quickened, the heat between her thighs mounting to an unbearable pitch. As though he knew, he touched her there, just once, and she rocketed into a climax that made her cry out his name in shocked abandon.

Boneless, she collapsed against him. "I never—that didn't…"

"There's more," he said fiercely and swept her into his arms, carrying her the length of the room into a vast bedroom. He laid her on her back on the king-size bed, covering her with his body, kissing her breasts, her shoulders, her mouth, giving her no mercy where none was needed. Then he reached down and ripped her suit from her hips.

After kicking off her shoes, Lia tugged the turquoise fabric from her legs and feet, only wanting to be naked for him; within her, something never touched before rose and broke at the wonder in his face as he took in the length of her slender body. She said unsteadily, "It's only me."

"You're so beautiful. So generous and brave."

The look on his face made her want to cry. This was about lust, she thought frantically. Only lust. "Seth," she said forcefully, "you've got too many clothes on."

His green eyes blazed at her. "Take your mask off," he said. "Please."

She bit her lip, feeling herself weaken at this passionate pleading from a man, she'd be willing to bet, who rarely begged for anything. "I've shown you too much already," she cried. "We have one night, Seth, just one night. But one night can be a lifetime, you understand that as well as I do."

She couldn't tell him who she was. Because Seth Talbot, she knew this in her bones, had the power to change her life.

From the time she was five, when her first violin had been put in her arms, she'd worked single-mindedly toward one goal: to be one of the best in the world. She wasn't there yet. With the humility of the true artist, she knew she had a long way to go. She'd also discovered in the last hour or so that a man called Seth Talbot could totally derail her. Distract her from her ambitions, from all she'd studied and practiced and longed for.

She couldn't afford to have that happen. No one was going to do that to her.

"I'll give you anything you ask but my identity," she said in a low voice.

He stood up in a surge of raw energy, pulling off his leather boots and dark trousers. "Anything?" he snarled. "Are you sure of that?"

"Yes," she said, refusing to back down. "I'm sure."

His body entranced her with its hard planes and flow of muscle. She rose to her knees, the light from the open windows catching on the sequins of her mask. Leaning forward, she very delicately tongued his nipple, hearing his harsh gasp of pleasure over the thrumming of blood in her ears. Then she clasped him by the hips, burying his arousal in the soft valley between her breasts. He threw back his head, thrusting into her, then suddenly pushing her back to fall on top of her on the bed.

"I can't think of anything but wanting you," he gasped, laving her breasts and belly with hands and tongue, then moving lower to push her thighs open. She was all too ready for him, wet, hot and slick.

"I can't believe I—" she began, then forgot everything as

again he overpowered her, sending her, sobbing his name, to topple over the edge. But even then he didn't let up. From a long way away, she felt him ease between her legs, felt that first hard push and enveloped him as if he'd been made for her, and her alone.

His silken thrusts, her own heated welcome…she writhed beneath him, out of control, beyond herself, in a joining that she couldn't have resisted to save her soul. Possessiveness, primitive and furious, drove her upward until his elemental rhythms were her own.

She heard him cry out sharply, saw his face convulse, and felt deep within her the strength and surrender of his release. Her own followed inexorably, throwing her against him as waves dash themselves against the cliffs.

Utterly spent, Lia drew him down to lie over her. His forehead dug her mask into her cheek even as his breath cooled her throat. When she could find her voice, she whispered, "I've never in my life felt anything like that."

"Neither have I."

Part of her wanted to toss off a joke, to make light of a mating that had thrown all her preconceptions of herself into disarray. But she knew she'd regret it if she did; for this mating was not to be defused so easily. "So for you it was different, too?"

"Couldn't you tell?"

"I'm not exactly experienced."

"My second name is control," he said tightly, raising his head to look straight through the slits in her mask into her eyes. "But I lost it. Totally. With you."

What was she supposed to say to that? For she believed him without a sliver of doubt. Trust, indeed, Lia thought with a quiver of panic. How could she trust a man she'd only met an hour ago? Trust was the word on which friendships were based. Not one-night stands. "So did I," she mumbled. "Lose it, I mean."

"I noticed," he said dryly.

She gave him the faintest of smiles. "Perhaps we could go a little slower next time?"

"Your guess is as good as mine," he said harshly. "If there's one thing I've learned in the last hour, it's not to anticipate as far as you're concerned. A useless exercise."

Suddenly intensely curious, Lia said, "You must have had a lot of women...I don't see how I'm so different."

"I've never gone from woman to woman, that's not the way I operate. Nor do I ever allow a woman to get too close. You're different because I had no choice."

His expression was inimical. With a shiver along her spine, she said, "That's what's so frightening—neither did I."

"Right now, I want you again," he said with passionate intensity. "I want to take my time, explore every inch of your body and learn what pleases you—I want to put my seal on you so you'll never forget me."

"Seth," she said quietly, "I'll never forget you."

Lines of frustration scoring his cheeks, he said, "But you won't tell me who you are."

"You know more about me than anyone else in the world!" she said with explosive truth. "You've got to be content with that."

"We'll see," he said, and ran his hand down her hip. "Your skin's so silky, so smooth...like the inside of a shell." He took the tip of her breast between his fingers, gently tugging on it. "You like that, don't you?"

"Yes," she breathed, seeking his mouth with hers, "I like that."

He carried her with him, caress by caress, and each one, she would have sworn, was imbued with tenderness and the simple wish to give her pleasure. With an answering tenderness she traced collarbone, rib and hipbone, kissed muscle and flank, then finally encircled his arousal, watching his eyes darken and hearing his breath quicken. "Not so fast," he gasped, lifting her to straddle him, his hands spanning her waist as the light of a Parisian moon fell white on her skin.

She slipped over him like a glove, her eyes closed as he entered her more and more fully, until she was filled with him. Then he drew her body down in a lissome curve until her breast was in his mouth. Sheer delight transfixing her, Lia buried her fingers in the tangle of blond hair on his chest and threw back her head. This time her climax came as slowly as the heat of a summer day rises with the dawn; her heart began to race against his palm. Not until then did Seth start moving deep within her, long, slow strokes that drove her closer and closer to the edge.

With exquisite timing he waited for his own release until the sharp cries of completion were breaking from her lips. As she rode him, her own excitement like a goad, he rose to meet her and fell with her into that abyss that was both a presage of death and the joy of rebirth.

This time it was Lia who fell on top of Seth, her mask digging into his chest. Part of her wanted to rip it off just because it was uncomfortable; part of her longed to rid herself of it so that he could see her eyes, stunned and slumberous with fulfillment.

But she mustn't. She couldn't. She had a life outside this room. She'd lose any ability to focus on that life if she allowed Seth Talbot to become part of it; she wouldn't even be able to pick up her violin, let alone tune it.

She couldn't toss away something that had been her sole purpose for seventeen years just because of one man. Just because his green eyes with their darts of gold fire had cast a spell over her.

"Are you all right?" Seth said gently, his arm tightening around her in a way she could only interpret as possessive.

She strove to find her voice. To move back from a place

where she'd turned into a stranger, a woman whose existence she'd never suspected. "Yes. No. You sure ask complicated questions."

He chuckled, a deep reverberation in his chest. "You flatter me."

"Believe me, this has nothing to do with flattery."

"So you like making love with me."

"There's no need to fish for compliments, Seth Talbot. *Like* nowhere near approximates how you make me feel. But do you know what?"

"I couldn't possibly guess."

"I didn't have any supper, because I was going to eat at the ball. I'm hungry."

"For food? When you've got me?"

"Yep," she chuckled. "Sorry about that."

He sat up, pulling her with him. "There's a wonderful invention called room service. What would you like?"

His smile had warmed those remarkable green eyes. Was she mad to think tenderness was the emotion behind that warmth? A tenderness that curled gentle fingers around her heart. She said hastily, "Seafood crêpes and surprise me with dessert."

"Done," he said. He reached for the phone, spoke rapidly into it in impeccable French, and replaced the receiver. Standing up, he stretched with lazy sensuality. "I feel great."

"You look better than great," she said primly, "and shouldn't you put something on before you answer the door?"

"Wouldn't want to shock the management." He disappeared in the direction of the bathroom. Moments later he came back with two white robes, monogrammed in gold on the pockets with the insignia of the hotel. "One for you," he said, tossing it in her lap. His voice deepened. "I don't want anyone but me seeing your beauty."

I want to put my seal on you...wasn't that what he'd said?

She couldn't handle such possessiveness; yet didn't the mere thought of him with another woman spur her with a hot jab of jealousy?

Explain that, Lia, she thought; and knew she couldn't.

CHAPTER THREE

LIA lifted the soft white folds of the robe to her face so that her breasts—which she'd always thought were rather too full—were hidden from Seth. "Beauty?" she repeated. "My body's okay. But it's not—"

"You're exquisite," he said shortly.

"Oh," said Lia, knowing she was blushing under her mask and makeup. "Not much point in arguing with that tone of voice."

"None whatsoever. I get the feeling you haven't had many compliments in your life."

Her parents, wrapped up in their own careers, had each had extraordinarily high standards. They'd dispensed advice when they'd thought of it, but little in the way of praise. Lionel, with whom she'd had that short-lived affair, had been too self-absorbed to bother with compliments. As for her music, it was only lately that the critics had started noticing her. A few had doled out cautious doses of praise; and how she'd hungered for that, she thought with uncomfortable truth.

"You've gone a long way away," Seth said.

With a tiny jolt Lia came back to the present. To a man who demanded the truth from her, just as the violin did. She said irritably, tracing the gold monogram with one finger, "You shake me up…and I don't just mean sexually."

Because her head was downbent, she didn't see how his eyes sharpened, nor how intently they were studying her. "Good," he said. "Ah, there's the door. I'll be right back."

She heard the murmur of voices from the other room, then Seth wheeled a mahogany trolley covered with starched white linen into the bedroom. He whipped off the coverings with a flourish, and within moments she was sitting beside him in bed, balancing a Limoges plate on a tray. The crêpes looked and smelled delicious. *"Bon appétit,"* she said, and tucked in with gusto.

Seth poured her a glass of chilled Chardonnay from one of the most famous of French châteaux; again she was unaware of how watchful his eyes were as she ate and drank, enjoying each mouthful. After she'd wiped the last drop of the luscious, velvety sauce from her plate with a piece of crunchy baguette, he removed the silver cover from a platter of French pastries.

Lia's eyes widened. "They're works of art. Oh look, perfect little swans filled with whipped cream…I'll have one of those."

She let her teeth sink into the delicately crunchy puff pastry; the cream was flavored with Grand Marnier. "I've died and gone to heaven," she pronounced.

"So I have a rival already."

She laughed, dabbed some cream on his chin and leaned over to lick it off with deliberate seductiveness. "Can't I have the swans as well as you?"

He passed her a glazed strawberry embedded in *crème anglaise* and the lightest of pastry. "You have an appetite for life, little butterfly."

Lia licked more cream from her fingers. "Life is meant to be lived," she said grandly.

"You're what—twenty? Twenty-one? And only one bed partner until tonight? That's not what I'd call living life to the full."

"I'm twenty-two years old and I'm interested in things other than sex," she retorted. "Don't let's argue, Seth, I'm having too much fun."

"What things? What do you do with yourself when you're not going to masked balls?"

Subconsciously, hadn't she been expecting his curiosity to surface? Her chin defiantly tilted, she said, "I'm not asking you what you do for your living, and I don't want you asking me—you promised you wouldn't pry."

"I own and run Talbot Holdings. Ever heard of them?"

Her hands had stilled. "Tal-Air?" she said. He nodded. "I often fly with your company. The planes are on time, the seats are comfortable and the staff friendly."

"We try," Seth said, adding easily, "so you fly a lot?"

She'd been stupid to have volunteered that scrap of personal information. "Not a lot," Lia said coolly. "Do you own Tal-Oil as well?"

He nodded. "Along with a line of tankers and cruise ships."

"This suite makes more sense," she said, and took the last mouthful of her pastry. "As do the swans. You're a very rich man." On purpose she made this sound, subtly, like an insult.

Seth bit into a chocolate éclair. "Belgian chocolate," he said amiably. "Want some?"

His change of subject threw her. As he'd probably intended. "Is Paris for lovers?" she rejoined, and rested her hand on his as she bit into the smooth, rich chocolate.

"So are we making love or war?" he asked with deliberate provocation.

"You tell me."

He lifted the tray from her lap, swung his feet down and pulled her to her feet. "Come with me—I want to show you the balcony."

His hand was tugging her along, the hand that had explored her body with such devastating intimacy. In her bare feet Lia padded across what felt like an acre of carpet. Seth swung open the doors and she stepped outside into massed potted flowers, the cool of night and the magic of this most magical of cities. Behind them sighed the unending traffic from Rue de Rivoli; past Jardin des Tuileries lay the river Seine; the lights of the Latin quarter and Les Invalides spangled the sky. Lia gave a sigh of pure happiness. "Glorious," she whispered.

"Glorious," he agreed, turned her hard in his arms and jammed her against the wall. Her robe slipped from her shoulder as his own fell open. Then they were kissing each other as though they'd never mated so passionately in the bed indoors. Skin to skin, heat to heat, desire igniting desire, until Seth lifted her bodily as though she weighed no more than a butterfly. Lia wrapped her thighs tight around him, panting with need, pushing her hips into his first hard thrust. As her climax ripped through her, Seth groaned deep in his chest, throbbing deep within her, emptying himself.

Slowly Lia returned to reality. The stone wall was digging into her back. Her feet were cold. "Even in Paris, we could be arrested for that," she croaked.

"Then we'd better go inside," he said, and carried her through the doors into the green and silver luxury of the bedroom.

"I need to lie down," she mumbled, her face buried in his chest. Would she ever forget the scent of his skin? Her own skin was suffused with it. He had indeed put his seal on her, she thought in a flash of terror.

When he reached the bed, he put her down with a gentleness that made her eyes sting with tears. If she'd been honest, she'd have told him it was love they'd been making all night, not war. But she didn't want to go near the word *love*. Not with Seth. "Hold onto me," she said raggedly, scarcely knowing what she was asking for.

Swiftly he lay down beside her, gathering her into his arms

and drawing her into the warmth of his long body. She melted into him, knowing with complete certainty that she wanted to make love to him again…in a minute, when she'd caught her breath.

With the suddenness of a very small child, Lia fell asleep.

She woke to night and the instant remembrance of where she was. Someone, Seth she could only presume, had drawn the heavy damask curtains over the windows; a soft glow from a nightlight in the bathroom was the room's only illumination.

Seth. Who'd ravished her, body and soul.

He was curled into her back, his breath wafting her bare shoulder. He was, she could tell, deeply asleep. She twisted in his arms, her eyes adjusting to the darkness. His face, in sleep, was both full of strength and yet undeniably vulnerable in a way that touched her to the heart. She looked away and knew with every fiber of her being that she had to get out of here. Away from him.

While there was still time.

Moving as carefully as she could, she eased his arm off her ribs and shifted toward the edge of the bed. Her bodysuit was draped over a Louis XVII chair, her shoes neatly aligned on the carpet nearby. She'd dropped all three of them on the floor all those hours ago. So Seth hadn't fallen asleep as quickly as she.

Had perhaps watched her as she slept.

Taking her clothes, Lia crept into the bathroom. Her makeup was smeared, her body a flow of pale curves in the long mirrors. She dragged on the bodysuit, struggling with the zipper, the wings drooping forlornly from the sleeves. The costume no longer looked outrageous: merely silly. Picking up her shoes, she tiptoed across the expanse of parquet toward the big double doors that led to safety.

Seth's cloak had been thrown carelessly over a delicate antique table by the door. She grabbed the cloak with deep relief and swathed herself in its dark folds. Then, her pulse racketing in her ears, Lia slid the door open, slipped through and closed it as quietly as she could.

Quickly she traveled the length of the hallway toward the red Exit sign. After jamming her feet into her pretty sandals, she ran down several flights of stairs, emerging in the front lobby. The concierge had his back to her. The doorman opened the glass door with impeccable courtesy, asking if she'd like a taxi.

"Non, merci," she said with a distracted smile, and walked down the street as though she made a habit of leaving luxurious hotels in the dark hours before dawn.

No coach, she thought wildly. No pumpkin, either.

Cinderella had only danced with the prince. Not made impassioned love to him…how many times had it been?

Early roses were blooming in the gardens, their fragrance languorously sweet. The half-moon had sunk in the sky. A taxi whipped past, and a scooter. Lia turned a corner, then doubled back on herself, knowing at some subliminal level that it was essential she cover her tracks.

The cloak had a hood. She drew it over her head and hurried along the deserted streets, taking the most circuitous of routes to Mathieu's flat in the 8th *arrondissement.* Mathieu had left for a concert tour. His key was in the tiny pocket in her bodysuit; its small metal outline felt immensely comforting against her thigh.

Thirty minutes later Lia was inside the flat, her heart racing from climbing the five flights of wooden stairs. Once inside, she looked around with the air of a woman who wasn't entirely sure where she was.

Or whether she wanted to be here.

Mathieu believed in minimalism. White walls, black leather chairs, three black and white photographs over his expensive stereo equipment: as different from Seth's luxuriously decorated suite as a space could be.

Seth. She mustn't think about Seth. She couldn't afford to. She had a rehearsal in Stockholm at four this afternoon, a concert tonight. Her flight left from Orly early this morning.

In the bathroom, it took Lia several minutes to take off her mask, which she'd anchored with glue just over each ear. But finally she was free of it. She then scrubbed the last of her makeup from her face and unpinned her hair so it tumbled to her shoulders. Taking off her bodysuit, she packed it, along with the mask and shoes, in the box the rental shop had given her. In a move that she was now hugely grateful for, she'd affixed the correct postage yesterday evening before she'd left for the ball. She could mail the box on her way to the airport.

Because she'd been so hungry for anonymity, she'd given a false name at the rental shop. They could keep the deposit, she thought. It was a cheap price to pay to preserve her privacy.

To keep her safe from Seth, when he came after her? He would, wouldn't he? He hadn't become the head of a vast international network of planes, ships and oil companies by sitting back and letting the world come to him.

She was thinking about him again. She'd sworn she wasn't going to do that. Knowing she should hurry, Lia walked, naked, back into the bathroom. The mirror was a sleek rectangle, edged with cold, unforgiving chrome. In it she saw a woman she no longer knew. Her features were the same, the lustrous black hair and dark brown eyes, legacy of her Italian father; her high cheekbones and winged brows, her long, slim body, all gifts of her Norwegian mother.

It was everything else that had changed.

As though she couldn't help herself, Lia lifted her palm to her nostrils, and caught, elusively, the scent of Seth's skin. As pain washed over her, she closed her eyes, conjuring him up, remembering with frightening clarity all the gifts of his body, the turbulence in his green eyes as he came to climax.

He'd entered her. Physically, of course. But more than that, he'd invaded her soul.

Biting her lip, she turned on the shower and stepped inside, grabbing the soap and lathering herself. Surely if she washed Seth from her skin, she could as easily wash him from her memory.

He was a man. Just a man. She'd never see him again.

Hadn't she taken every precaution she could to ensure that was true?

Not yet fully awake, Seth reached across the bed for his butterfly lover. He'd fallen asleep with his arms wrapped around her, knowing that what he wanted most in the world was to wake up with her beside him. In the daylight, he'd find out who she was. She'd understand as clearly as he did that they couldn't simply go their separate ways...

Where was she?

His eyes flew open. Morning light gleamed through chinks in the curtains. Other than himself, the bed was empty.

Her bodysuit was gone from the chair.

Seth shoved himself up on one elbow, ears straining for the slightest sound; and heard only the distant roar of traffic far below. He surged out of bed. Her shoes were gone, too.

Naked as the day he was born, his heart like a cold lump in his chest, he strode into the bathroom. Blankly, his own face stared back at him from the mirror. He turned away from it. The vast living room was deserted. His cloak was gone from the table by the door.

Far beyond pride, he searched every surface in the suite for a note, and found nothing.

She'd gone. Without a trace.

Like a man stunned, Seth walked back into the bedroom

and sank down on the bed. The trolley was still there, the left-over pastries looking nowhere near as appetizing as they had the night before. He remembered with aching clarity how she'd sunk her teeth into them, then licked cream from his chin, her lips a voluptuous curve… With an inarticulate groan, Seth lowered his head into his hands. How could he have been so stupid as to fall asleep? To let her escape?

He didn't know the first thing about her. Not her name, or her occupation, not even what she looked like under that glamorous, all-concealing mask.

The mask she'd refused to remove.

He could scarcely fault her. She'd done exactly what she'd said she'd do—make love to him for one night and then vanish.

As though he'd meant nothing to her.

He dug his fingers into his forehead, forcing himself to recognize the single, dangerous mistake he'd made, out of pride and overweening arrogance. All evening and far into the night, he'd been convinced that he could change her mind. That sooner or later, she'd rip off her mask and tell him her name.

She hadn't done either one. Instead she'd waited until he was asleep, then fled.

How dare she have left him as though what had happened between them was of no more consequence than a game of cards or a few drinks at a bar?

He got up, marched over to the windows and ripped back the curtains. Sunlight streamed through the panes, making him wince. Far on the horizon, the Eiffel Tower gleamed like a needle in the light.

It should have been raining. A sky dark with thunderclouds, wind scudding through the wet streets.

Sure, he thought, and with the smallest glimmer of humor knew he was being ridiculous. So she'd gone. So what? She was a woman. Just a woman. The world was full of them, and he'd never had the slightest trouble finding one to warm his bed.

But not one of them had ever touched him in the places he'd been touched last night. In his heart. His soul.

He'd never allowed them to. Never wanted them to. But from the moment he'd seen the woman in the turquoise body-suit, he'd had no choice. In a way he didn't understand—and bitterly resented—she'd pierced every one of his defenses.

And now she'd run away. Leaving him more alone than he'd ever been in his life.

CHAPTER FOUR

SETH hit his palm hard against the window frame, the sudden pain bringing him to his senses. He was going to shower and get dressed. Then he'd get on the phone and have her traced, his mysterious lover in the feathered mask.

She'd have left a trail. Everyone did.

He'd find her. Sooner or later, and he had the money to pay for sooner. Then he'd tell her exactly what he thought of her for sneaking off under cover of darkness, like a common thief.

His eyes suddenly widened, his hand gripping the window frame with vicious strength. Godalmighty, he thought. Protection. I didn't use any. I never even thought of it.

He'd broken one of his cardinal rules.

How many times had they made love? Three? And not once had it occurred to him to get out the foil packets he kept in his suitcase.

She hadn't mentioned protection, either. In a surge of relief he realized she must have been on the Pill. Most modern women were. Took it for granted.

But she hadn't had a lover in three years. Why would she be on the Pill?

She was an intelligent woman, far too intelligent to get into a stranger's bed without taking precautions against pregnancy.

He considered himself of more than average intelligence.

But last night he'd been thinking with his hormones, not his brains. Why should she be any different?

Again he pounded his fist against the window, trying to stop the desperate seesawing of his thoughts. He'd just have to pray that she wasn't pregnant. From the time he'd been old enough to think about it, he'd never had any intention of causing a child of his to enter the world. His parents had rid him of that particular desire many years before.

Along with so much else.

He wasn't going to think about his parents. Not at—he glanced at the bedside clock—seven in the morning, when he'd had no more than four hours sleep. Decisively Seth marched into the bathroom, showered the last traces of the night from his body, and dressed in a pinstriped suit with a custom-made blue shirt and a silk tie. His Italian leather shoes, thanks to the hotel staff, gleamed like polished glass.

He was no longer in the garb of a highwayman. Although he still felt like one. Picking up the phone, Seth got to work.

Twenty minutes later, he'd covered all the angles. He'd talked to the concierge, the doorman and the manager, none of whom had been of the slightest use. He'd then contacted a professional investigator, ordering him to alert taxis, buses and the Métro; to phone every last place in the city that rented costumes; and to advertise very discreetly for anyone who'd seen a woman on the streets of Paris after 3:00 a.m. wearing a long black cloak over a turquoise butterfly costume.

Seth could have contacted all these sources himself. But he was too well known, and the last thing he wanted was the press getting hold of this. It was too private. Too personal. Too close to the bone.

He might be desperate to find her. But he couldn't splash her image over every newspaper in Europe.

Putting down the phone, he scowled at the ormolu clock

sitting sedately on the carved marble mantel. Now all he could do was wait. Wait and hope.

He left the suite and ran downstairs to the waiting limo. He was going to focus on the job at hand, he told himself forcefully as he hurried outside into the spring sunshine. Business as usual.

Some high-powered negotiations, followed by a meeting with his Paris staff, took up the whole day. Seth finally left the office at seven-thirty and walked to his favorite café on the Champs-Elysées, loosening his tie as he went. Snagging a table on the sidewalk, he ordered coquelet and crème brûlée, two of the house specialties. Then he took out his cell phone and punched in the investigator's number.

Five minutes later, his face set, he put down the phone and took a big gulp of an excellent merlot. The investigator had located the shop that had rented the turquoise costume; but the woman who'd chosen it had been wearing dark glasses and an all-concealing floppy hat, and had given a false name and address.

This dead end had been accompanied by many others. No one, it seemed, had seen anyone in a long black cloak on foot, in a taxi, on a bus, on the Métro, at an airport or in a hotel. In terms of concrete information Seth had gained exactly nothing. *Rien.* Zero. Zilch.

His butterfly had disappeared from the face of the earth.

No, he thought slowly. He'd learned a little more than nothing. She'd disguised herself and given a false name when she'd rented the costume, which was well before she'd met Seth. Why had she done that?

She must in some way be famous. Her name so well known, at least locally, that she didn't want her actions traced.

That really narrowed the field, Seth thought sarcastically. Now all he had to look for was a famous young woman who loved to eat French pastries at midnight and whose naked body he could have described in embarrassing detail.

Nothing to it.

One thing was sure. She wasn't after his money.

Which differentiated her from most of the people he met.

A plate of thinly sliced rare meat decorated with julienned carrots and *haricots* was put in front of him, and his wineglass topped up. Blindly Seth stared at the food. His appetite had deserted him; a chunk of ice had congealed in his gut and his hands were as cold as if this were winter, not a warm spring evening.

What if he never saw her again?

Three weeks later, striding along Broad Street on his way to his broker, Seth suddenly stopped dead in his tracks. Two men cannoned into him; he muttered an apology and stepped to one side of the pavement.

That was her—wasn't it?

A leggy blonde in a chocolate-brown Chanel suit had stepped out from between two of the massive Corinthian columns of the New York Stock Exchange. Something in the confidence with which she was looking up and down the street was irresistibly familiar. Then, as if she sensed him staring at her, she turned around.

Too tall. Too thin. The angle of her jaw all wrong.

She gave Seth the once-over with a calculation she didn't bother to hide, and said with a smile that masterfully combined interest with hauteur, "Can I help you?"

"Thanks, no—I thought you were someone else," Seth said.

"Have we met before?"

Oh, yeah, he thought, underneath that patrician glaze you're definitely interested. "No. My apologies for bothering you," he said, smiled at her with no particular sincerity and walked away.

He'd made a fool of himself. Again. How many times in the last twenty-one days had he seen a woman whom he'd been convinced was his butterfly lover? Who'd left his heart pounding in his chest and his body irradiated with hope?

The only place it hadn't happened had been on a recent trip to the slums of Rio de Janeiro. He'd gone there as the new president, treasurer and, so far, sole member of the philanthropic foundation he was setting up, as a way of figuring out how best he could give away some of his money. He'd been too devastated by what he'd seen in Rio to be on the lookout for a woman of any age or shape.

Back home, the story was different: he'd been unable to forget that single, tumultuous night in Paris.

In the course of those few impassioned hours, had he fallen in love? Surely not! If, as a much younger man, he'd sworn off having children, he'd even more strongly vowed to avoid such romantic claptrap. Falling in love was for teenagers. Not for a man like himself with a family fortune and the driving ambition to quadruple that fortune.

To show his mother and father that he didn't need their money? Or their love?

Allan, his ineffectual, unhappy father, and Eleonore, his mother, with her cold will of steel: Seth felt equally distant from both of them.

Eleonore wanted Seth married to a woman of her choice, someone who would present no threat to her authority. His butterfly lover wouldn't do, for sure. Too beautiful, too sexy, too intelligent and much too strong-willed.

Not that Seth wanted to get married. He never had.

He wasn't in love. He was in lust. A very different thing. Instead of mooning after the unattainable, he should start dating again. Find himself a sophisticated blonde who'd demand nothing more of him than he was willing to give.

Like the woman by the stock exchange?

She was the last woman he wanted.

Fuming inwardly, Seth took the granite steps of his broker's building two at a time and for the next hour and a half focused his mind on the risks of commodities and the vagaries of currency exchanges. Then he went home to his brownstone near Central Park, and stripped off his work clothes. He hauled on shorts and a tank top, lacing his sneakers with vicious strength.

Enough, he thought, as he stepped on his treadmill and adjusted the slope. He wasn't going to let a snip of a woman ruin his life. So she'd vanished. Good riddance to her. If she'd gotten under his skin this much in one night, imagine what she'd have done if he'd continued seeing her. He was well rid of her.

He was going to get his life back on track and forget about her. If by any chance he ever saw her again, he'd run like hell in the opposite direction.

Not that he would see her. She'd made sure of that.

Holding fast to his anger, because he liked it a whole lot better than the agonies of regret he'd been suffering ever since that night in a Paris hotel, Seth turned up the speed on the treadmill and started to jog. He was indeed back on track, he thought with a grim smile.

With the past where it belonged. In the past.

And the woman of mystery where she belonged. Out of his life.

Locking her fingers in her lap to control their trembling, Lia stared at the thin blue line. It was the second time in as many days that she'd used the pregnancy test, and it was the second time it had turned out positive.

The first time, she'd convinced herself it was a false positive. She couldn't be pregnant. She just couldn't be.

But this evening she could no longer muster such certitude. The evidence was staring her in the face.

She was carrying Seth's baby.

Suddenly and unexpectedly, joy flooded her. She would

bear the child of a man who'd brought her felicity beyond her imagining, and who'd aroused in her a passion she hadn't known she possessed. Hugging her belly in instinctive protection, she grinned at the opposite wall, her dark eyes luminous with happiness.

She was going to be a mother.

Then, with a jolt, the hard voice of reason asserted itself. Lia's smile vanished. She was seven weeks pregnant by a man she'd vowed never to see again.

Unable to sit still any longer, Lia walked over to one of the two small windows in her bachelor flat. This one looked out on the iron balconies of the neighboring apartment block; the afternoon sun shone hot on the bricks. She was pregnant with Seth Talbot's child. Seth, who ran a host of international companies from his headquarters a mere thirty blocks from here, and who was listed in Fortune magazine as one of the richest men in America.

Well done, Lia.

In two days she was flying to New Zealand to take part in a festival of young musicians. In a wave of panic Lia felt the tidy rows of bricks blur in front of her eyes. How could she fit a baby into her life? She couldn't. It was impossible. She had concerts booked as far ahead as three years from now; and her career was taking off in a way that both exhilarated and challenged her. She couldn't abandon it for motherhood.

Abortion?

Everything in her cried out in repudiation. Seth's child? She'd never be able to live with herself. Besides, she was responsible for this baby's existence: Seth hadn't forced himself on her. She'd gone willingly to his bed and now was paying the consequences.

Seth was also responsible.

So what was she supposed to do? Phone him up at work

and say, "Remember me? The woman you had torrid sex with in Paris? Guess what, I'm pregnant."

She couldn't imagine doing that. Wouldn't he assume she was trying to trick him into marriage? He was a very rich man, and it was one of the oldest gambits in the book.

Oh God, she thought in despair, what was she going to do?

Go to the doctor. Find out for sure she was pregnant. Then she'd have the long flight to Auckland to sit quietly and consider her options.

She'd been right to worry, when she'd first met Seth, that he could derail her life.

He had. By making her pregnant.

Two weeks later, Lia sealed two identical letters, one addressed to Seth at his Manhattan headquarters, the other to an address in the Hamptons that she'd found on the Internet. The Hamptons boasted beachside homes for the extremely rich; she could only assume it was his retreat from the city. She was almost sure he must have a Manhattan address; but he would, of course, guard it from general knowledge. She, of all people, understood the value of personal privacy.

The decision she'd come to over the last few days was that she owed Seth the truth about her pregnancy: for pregnant she was, the doctor having merely confirmed something she'd already known.

Yet she dreaded him getting the letters. She couldn't bear to tarnish that magical night in Paris with accusations that she'd neglected to warn him she was unprotected against pregnancy; or, worse, with suspicions that she'd planned the whole thing to entrap him into marriage.

Whatever his reaction would be, she was sure of two things: it would be forceful and it would be disruptive. The owner of a company as far-reaching as Talbot Holdings hadn't gotten there by being nice. Lia got up from her desk, carrying the letters, took the stairwell to street level and pushed open the door. The July heat hit her like a blow, and for a moment she wavered, attacked by the dizziness that so far was her only symptom; she had, to her enormous relief, avoided morning sickness.

With a sense of putting herself in the hands of fate, Lia pushed away from the wall, walked two blocks and thrust the letters through the slot in the mailbox. There. She'd done it. The rest was up to Seth.

CHAPTER FIVE

LIA lay back on the chaise longue. Over her head, palm trees rattled their fronds in the warm Caribbean tradewinds, while a torrent of bougainvillea spangled her with shadows. On the blindingly white beach only a few feet from her private cottage, waves splashed gently up and down. Another kind of music, she thought idly. One she didn't have to work for.

Heaven. Utter heaven. How often did she lie back and do absolutely nothing?

Never was the short answer.

She'd get up soon and shower, put on her jazzy new sundress and wander to the least formal of the three restaurants that the resort boasted. Tomorrow afternoon, after a morning snorkeling on the reef, she had an appointment at the spa.

So what if the few days she was spending here were straining her budget to the breaking point? She'd gotten off-season rates, and only once a year did she treat herself to time spent entirely on her own.

She'd been here just over seven hours, and already she felt like a new woman. Just wait until tomorrow, she thought. A massage, a pineapple scrub and a dip in the thalassotherapy pool. Whatever that was.

She was quite willing to find out.

Lazily she got up from her chair and wandered toward her charming, air-conditioned cottage, which was nestled in a miniature botanical garden where brightly hued butterflies lit on the blooms, opening and closing their wings as they feasted on nectar. Lia stood on the stone walk, watching them for a moment. So careless, so hungry for the world's sweetness... once she'd been like that. But she'd changed in the last eight years.

How could she not have?

Ruefully she smiled at the iridescent turquoise patches on the wings of the nearest butterfly. After that night in Paris, it had been years before she could bring herself to wear turquoise again. But now she did. In fact, her new swimsuit was also iridescent turquoise, and fit her like a glove.

She looked very good in it, she thought smugly, and went indoors to change.

She was going to have a wonderful time here. All on her own.

Seth scowled at his reflection in the mirror of his cottage. He looked godawful. He certainly looked like he could do with a good dose of R&R. What better place to get it than at the White Cay Resort?

He picked up his razor, running it over his face. The wound that furrowed his ribs was healing, although too slowly for his liking. It itched like crazy under the tape. If he could rid himself of the nightmares that all too often plagued his sleep, he'd be more or less okay.

Dinner, he thought. He wasn't in the mood for formality. The Tradewind Room would do fine for tonight. Nor was he in the mood for conviviality, so hopefully he wouldn't know anyone here. If he kept to himself for a couple of days, he could go back to the rat race refreshed.

He ran a comb through his thick blond hair and left the cottage, glancing with pleasure at the long stretch of pale sand

and the impossibly blue sea. But as he entered the foyer of the restaurant, his heart sank.

"Seth," Conway Fleming said cheerfully. "Wouldn't have expected to find you here—not enough action."

"I came here to get away from it," Seth said, not very tactfully.

Conway laughed heartily. "Don't we all! Do you know Pete Sonyard? Sonyard Yachts...and his wife Jeannine."

Seth dredged up what he knew about the builder of the world's fastest yachts, and discovered Jeannine was an authority on the history of the Caribbean islands. As for Conway, Seth had known him, off and on, for years; he was well regarded on Wall Street, and known as a serious patron of the arts. As the conversation gathered momentum, Seth started mentally rehearsing how he was going to get a table to himself.

Then he saw the woman.

She'd just pushed open the door to the foyer. She had on a brief red dress, her hair a silky fall of raven-black. Her legs were bare and slender, her feet in ridiculously high-heeled red sandals. Her skin seemed to glow in the warm rays of the setting sun.

She was incredibly beautiful.

She glanced behind her, then held the door wider for a mother and two little children to enter. The boy had black hair like hers. He looked up, asking her something; she crouched to answer him, taking off her dark glasses, the dress drawn tight across her thighs. The boy tugged at her hair. She said something that made him laugh, and glanced up at his mother, the line of her throat making Seth's heart thud in his chest.

How long since he'd felt such instant and imperative lust?

Too long. Much too long.

She and the two children made a delightful tableau, he thought painfully, and across the room heard her laugh. Husky. Undeniably sexy. As she stood up, smoothing her dress, his blood pressure jolted up another notch. The dress was sexy, too, all the more so for being so sophisticated. It was sleeveless, the neckline and armholes square-cut; just above the hem, small squares had been cut out of the fabric, hinting at the skin beneath.

With one final remark to the little family, the black-haired woman turned and headed for the Tradewind Room. She hadn't even glanced his way. Infuriated that the intensity of his gaze hadn't caused her to as much as turn her head, Seth heard Conway say, "Gorgeous, isn't she?"

"You know her?"

"Who doesn't?"

"I don't," Seth said. Her face and body were unforgettable, let alone her air of confidence and poise, along with the genuine warmth she'd shown the little boy. She was stunning, he thought, and knew he wanted to meet her very badly.

Maybe, finally, he'd gotten over that debacle of eight years ago.

"I'm surprised you've never run into her, Seth," Conway remarked. "You have an interest in classical music, don't you?"

Seth did. A fledgling, but very genuine passion for something he'd connected with only a couple of years ago, through his old friend Julian in Berlin. He frowned. "What's that got to do with it?"

"That's Lia d'Angeli," Conway replied. "Darling of audiences and critics alike—not to mention the press and the makers of CDs. I'll introduce you." Raising his voice, he called, "Lia?"

She looked over, saw Conway and smiled spontaneously. Her eyes were dark, Seth saw, almost as dark as her hair. Both her lips and her nails were a fire-engine red. It was a very generous and voluptuous mouth, he thought, his own dry. She said warmly, "Conway! How lovely to see you."

Lia had known Conway for nearly six years; his foundation in support of the arts had permitted her, four years ago, to purchase a Stradivarius violin, which had enriched her playing immeasurably. For Conway, she'd even give up her precious solitude. For one evening, anyway.

He leaned over and kissed her European fashion on both cheeks. "Let me introduce you to some friends of mine."

She glanced over at them, prepared to like them as much for Conway's sake as for their own, and heard him say, "Pete and Jeannine Sonyard, from Maine. And Seth Talbot, who's based in New York. Lia d'Angeli, the violinist."

Seth Talbot was standing there. Right in front of her. The late sun was gilding his blond hair, while his green eyes were fastened on her. The shock hit Lia with the force of a tidal wave. As the color drained from her face, the polished mahogany floor swayed and dipped under her feet. Seth, she thought frantically. It can't be. Oh God, get me out of here.

With all her strength she fought for control, willing the floor to stay firmly under her feet where it belonged. But to see him again, after so many years...briefly she closed her eyes, praying that she'd wake up and find this was nothing but a bad dream.

"Are you all right, Lia?" Conway asked in quick concern, taking her elbow in his hand.

"Yes...sorry. Too much sun today, I guess." With a huge effort she produced a smile for the Sonyards. "I flew from Helsinki to Toronto yesterday. A lot of dirty wet snow in Helsinki, and a downpour in Toronto—I don't recommend visiting either place in April. Do you blame me for lying out in the sun the minute I got here? But I must have overdone it."

She was babbling, she thought. Normally she rarely talked about the weather, there were too many other more interesting things to discuss. Jeannine laughed, making a commonplace remark about Maine's climate. Lia's eyes skidded sideways, met Seth's and winced away again.

He said with a pleasure that sounded entirely genuine, "I'm delighted to meet you, Signora d'Angeli. I have all seven of your CDs, and I've played them many times."

Shock and dismay were usurped by a torrent of rage that almost incapacitated Lia. How dare he act as though they'd never met before? As though she'd never written him two letters eight long years ago telling him about his impending fatherhood? "I'm flattered," she said with icy precision, and watched his jaw tighten at her rudeness. Deliberately allowing her voice to warm, she asked, "Conway, how long are you staying?"

Conway was looking understandably puzzled; he knew her well enough to have witnessed her unfailing courtesy to those who were interested in her playing. "Until tomorrow afternoon," he said. "You'll join us for dinner this evening?"

"I'd like that very much," Seth interposed.

You would, would you, Lia thought vengefully. Too bad. Not for one hundred Strads would she sit at the same table as Seth Talbot, whether they made small talk about the weather or discussed her *legato*. Because, of course, he'd now repudiated her twice. Eight years ago and right now. Just as if the two of them had never spent the night in each other's arms, and just as though she hadn't gotten pregnant as a result. She stretched her mouth in a smile that felt utterly false. "I'm afraid I must decline. I'm dining in the Reef Room tonight, I only came in here to look around."

Seth was looking at her quizzically. "We've never met, have we, Signora d'Angeli? I can't imagine how I've offended you."

She should have known he wouldn't take her bad manners lying down. Not the internationally known Seth Talbot, who in the last eight years had made more money than an entire orchestra earned in its lifetime. It was on the tip of her tongue to say sweetly, *But Mr. Talbot, have you forgotten how we*

made love on the balcony of a hotel in Paris? Or the two let-
ters I sent you afterward, mentioning the minor problem of
my pregnancy?

Although it would have given her great satisfaction to have
said all this, Lia bit the words back. If Seth Talbot wanted,
once again, to deny her existence, she should let him do so.
That way she'd keep him out of her life. Preserve her privacy,
as she'd done so strenuously for so long.

She said mendaciously, "I don't think we've ever met before, Mr. Talbot. But you remind me very strongly of someone I'd much prefer to forget…please forgive my lack of
good manners." There. She'd given an excuse for her rudeness without publicly embarrassing him by telling the truth.
Turning to Conway, she added, "I'd love to meet you tomorrow for breakfast, if you have the time."

Conway bowed gallantly. "I always have time for you, Lia.
Eight-thirty here in the foyer?"

"Wonderful," she said and smiled at the Sonyards. "Please
excuse me." Then she made the mistake of glancing at Seth. He
was staring at her, his brows knit, a look of such genuine puz-
zlement on his face that she could have slapped him. The man
should have been an actor, not the head of a giant corporation.

Calling on all her self-control, she said lightly, "I'm going
to be late for my reservation, I must go. Enjoy your evening."

"Until we meet again," Seth said in a clipped voice.

That'll be never if I have my way, thought Lia, turning on
her heel and leaving the foyer as though she had nothing more
important than dinner on her mind.

She didn't have a reservation in the Reef Room; she only
hoped they'd have room for her. Not that she was the slightest bit hungry.

Another wave of anger surged through her. Her heels tapping sharply on the stone path, she walked between banks of
plumbago, frangipani and hibiscus. Until Seth Talbot had

crossed her path, she'd been looking forward to her solitary meal in the Tradewind Room. How dare he act as though he'd never laid eyes on her before? How dare he? And then to have the gall to ask how he'd offended her. The bastard. The cold-hearted, irresponsible bastard.

Her steps faltered. It was her own child who was the bastard. Her beloved Marise.

Whose eyes were the green of a summer meadow. Just like Seth's.

Once Lia had realized, eight years ago, that Seth had no intention of answering her letters, she'd made it a policy never to speak about her personal life to the media; so Marise's existence, although generally known, only rarely emerged in print. She'd been fortunate in that she'd put on very little weight during her pregnancy, and had had a dressmaker who'd expertly masked the gentle bulge of Lia's belly with Empire waistlines and concealing panels of stiff fabric. She'd had to miss two concerts. That was all.

As her due date had approached, Lia had cashed in half the bonds her parents had left her and, using them as security, had bought a small, but very lovely old farm in the country eighty miles from Manhattan. The bank had come up with the mortgage and a local carpenter had done the renovations. Her daughter had been born in the little hospital five miles down the road.

She'd hired a nanny. She'd bought a car. She'd made a life for herself and her child. The farm had become home, giving mother and daughter a very necessary stability.

Despite his betrayal, she hadn't allowed Seth to derail her life. But neither had she been able to forget him. For one thing, every time she looked into her daughter's eyes, Lia saw him. For another, she'd never replaced him. Not once, in eight years, had she felt pulled toward a man the way she had been toward Seth. So her bed had remained empty, and her heart untouched.

Passion, once experienced in all its overwhelming power,

couldn't easily be duplicated. That had been one of the lessons Seth had taught her. That, along with the disillusion and wariness of the deeply wounded.

What was she going to do? She could leave the island tomorrow morning on the resort's helicopter, pleading a family emergency. Nancy, Lia's nanny, wouldn't be happy with her; it was vivacious, dependable Nancy who insisted Lia have a few days a year all to herself.

If she left, she wouldn't have to face Seth again. Breakfast with Conway, and then she'd be gone.

Seth was going to seek her out. He'd said as much, and he wasn't a man for idle words. How long would they be together before he spoke about the past? More important, how long could she keep her fury to herself?

Her fiery temper had gotten her into trouble more than once in the past. She couldn't risk it here, not with Seth. There was too much at stake. Because she wasn't going to let him near her daughter, not for anything. He'd done nothing to earn such a gift, and everything to desecrate it.

But if she ran for the farm with her tail between her legs, she'd be the loser. She needed this holiday desperately, for she was returning to a killer schedule of concerts and recording sessions. Why should she leave here just because Seth Talbot had turned up out of the blue?

He didn't want anything to do with her. If he had, he could have contacted her at any time in the last eight years.

Standing in the warmth of a Caribbean sunset, Lia snapped off a single bloom of hibiscus and defiantly tucked it behind her ear. She was going to march into the Reef Room as though she owned the place, and eat her way down the menu. Then she'd go to her cottage and read one of the books that had been sitting on her bedside table for the last six months.

Seth Talbot wasn't going to ruin her holiday.

But neither was he ever going to meet Marise.

CHAPTER SIX

A BIRD was screeching in the bushes next to the cottage. Seth turned over in bed and stared blearily at the clock radio. In bright red numerals it said 0545: numerals that were just as red as Lia d'Angeli's dress. Ouch, he thought, and buried his head under the pillows. The first bird had been joined by a second; it sounded like full-blown domestic warfare was being waged two feet from his open window.

He'd stake his brand new red Porsche that Lia had been planning on eating in the Tradewind Room until she'd seen him. Then she'd changed her mind *prestissimo*. He tried to block out the image of her crouched by the door, making a little boy laugh. Or the way her long black hair waved to her shoulders, gleaming like satin. Her skin was like satin, too, he thought, and felt his groin harden in instinctive response.

Trouble. That's what she spelled with her lustrous dark eyes and sensuous, red-painted mouth. Big trouble.

He didn't need that kind of trouble in his life. Why couldn't she have gone somewhere else for her holidays? Somewhere a long way from here.

Knowing sleep was out of the question, Seth turned on the bedside light and reached for the novel he'd started a couple of days ago. But he couldn't concentrate on the plot, and kept having to flick back through the pages to see who was who.

Impatiently he put the book down. It hadn't been the birds that had woken him; it had been a nightmare, one that seemed totally out of place in this luxurious setting.

The images were still fluttering at the edge of his vision: miserable shanties, burned villages, refugees displaced with only what they could carry on their backs. He'd seen it all only a few days ago in a rebel-torn area near Africa's equator. It was the children who had gotten to him. Orphaned children, weeping. Starving children beyond tears. A newly dead little boy, his mother wailing her sorrow…what were his troubles compared to that?

As always, he'd done his best to see that the money his foundation was channeling into the area went straight to those who needed it; in the course of which he'd run foul of a gun-happy rebel and a bullet had plowed across his ribcage. He was just lucky the guy's aim had been off.

No matter what he did, one thing was obvious. Single-handed or with the help of his admirable staff, he couldn't stop the war or stamp out the root causes of the poverty…those went far beyond the reach of one man, no matter how rich or how well-meaning.

Oddly enough, among Seth's primary emotions as he'd flown home had been a searing realization of the aridity of his own life. Sure, he had friends, good ones, scattered all over the globe. But otherwise, he was detached. Uninvolved. He could tell himself he was the inevitable product of the disastrous marriage between his mother and father. Blame his need to be a loner on them. But wasn't he, when all was said and done, poorer than any of those close-knit families he'd seen struggling to survive under a tropical sun? They at least had each other.

Who did he have?

No one. With a disgusted grunt, Seth heaved himself out of bed. Despite his sore ribs, he was going swimming. Afterward, so he wouldn't bump into Conway and Lia d'Angeli, he'd order room service: a calorie-laden breakfast of all the things that were bad for him, like bacon and hash browns. He needed this holiday and he was darn well going to enjoy it.

While the swim woke Seth up, breakfast made him drowsy, so he slept for nearly an hour in his lounge chair on the shaded, breezy deck of his cottage. Waking midmorning, he decided he had just enough time to join the boat that should be heading out to the reef for some snorkeling. Grabbing his gear, shoving his dark glasses on his nose, Seth set out for the dock.

The boat was ready to leave. Its sole occupant, other than the guide, was Lia d'Angeli, wearing a dazzlingly white cover-up over her swimsuit, her hair bundled under a wide-brimmed sunhat. Because she was chatting with the guide, she hadn't seen him.

He could change his mind. Hightail it back down the dock and bury his nose in his book. Peacefully, all by himself.

He didn't like backing down from anyone, least of all a woman.

Then his mind was made up for him. "Mornin', Mr. Talbot, sir," said the guide, a grin splitting his face. "You comin' with us this fine day?"

"Good morning," Seth said. "Yeah, thought I would."

In utter dismay Lia swiveled to face him. Seth Talbot was the last man she wanted to see this morning. He had cost her a very expensive dinner last night in the Reef Room, and he'd haunted her sleep. When Conway had brought his name up over breakfast, she'd changed the subject with a singular lack of grace. And now Seth was sauntering down the dock at the last minute to join an expedition she'd been very much looking forward to. Why couldn't he just leave her alone?

She said sarcastically, "What an unexpected pleasure."

"For both of us," he replied, mockery sparking his green eyes. "Surely you exaggerate."

The guide said amiably, "If you're both ready, we'll get going."

Although Lia could have jumped out of the boat and run for her life up the dock, a healthy dose of stubbornness was one of the attributes that had brought her success in a highly competitive field. "Hurry up, Seth," she said tightly, and watched him step into the dinghy, settling himself beside her on the thwart.

He was wearing a thin white T-shirt over lightweight shorts that doubled as swim trunks. His forearms were strongly muscled, his hands resting easily on his thighs...had she ever forgotten those long, lean fingers, the way they'd played her body as sensitively as any musician's? Like a lightning bolt, desire slammed through her and unconsciously Lia's body swayed toward him. Betraying her, just as he'd betrayed her so long ago.

No, she thought frantically. Not again.

Appalled, she straightened on the seat, holding herself rigid as the boat chugged away from the dock. The bow slapped the waves, the foam an effervescent white shot through with blue. Beautiful, she thought, trying with all her might to focus on anything other than the man sitting so close to her.

The small outboard motor was noisy, so at least she didn't have to talk to him.

All too soon, they reached the reef. The guide cut the motor. "Anyplace around here is good. We ask you not to touch the corals, it damages them, and some of them are poisonous." He gave another big grin. "I'll just sit here and wait for you...we got all the time in the world."

Lia bent to fasten her fins. Then, feeling absurdly self-conscious, she took off her white top. Her turquoise maillot, sleek-fitting, was low-cut front and back, and high-cut over her hips. She should be wearing a nun's habit, she thought irritably, not a swimsuit that exposed far more of her than it covered.

In spite of herself, she glanced over at Seth. His eyes were riveted on her, such raw hunger in them that she flinched away from him. So he felt it, too. After eight long years of silence, he still wanted her.

Her. Not her child.

Her temper flared to life, gloriously reviving. She'd been his victim years ago, when he hadn't answered her letters. But she didn't have to be anyone's victim right this minute. She was going to make him suffer. Unwise of her, no doubt, but understandable under the circumstances. She tossed her shirt across the forward thwart and leaned across him to get her mask, thereby giving him an unobstructed view of her cleavage. As she picked up the mask, she deliberately let her thigh brush his.

With a bland smile she watched him jolt on the seat, his jaw tightening, desire smoldering in those incredibly green eyes that Marise had inherited. Too bad, Seth Talbot, she thought meanly. There's not a hope in hell that I'll ever let you touch me again.

She said lightly, "Enjoy." After tucking her sunhat under her shirt on the thwart, Lia swung her legs over the edge of the dinghy and slipped into the sea. She rinsed her mask with water, fitted it over her face and swam away from the boat. Facedown, she was instantly transported to another world, where tiny fish flashed yellow, purple and black through a lacy network of indolently swaying coral.

Her heartbeat slowly settled back to normal, her anger subsiding. She shouldn't have thrust herself so blatantly at Seth when she had no intention of coming across. It had been crude of her. Crude and potentially dangerous.

But, she thought with a small smile, very satisfying.

Then she did her level best to put him out of her mind. He wasn't worth it. Nor was she going to allow him to ruin her precious and hard-earned holiday.

Seth had waited a couple of minutes before leaving the dinghy. He kept his T-shirt on, mostly because he couldn't stand advertising the wide strip of white plaster over his ribs. Bad enough to have stepped in the way of a stray bullet, without having to talk about it. Especially to the likes of Lia d'Angeli.

Who'd read his flare of lust like an open book and thrust her breasts practically in his face.

With an entirely predictable response on his part, he thought savagely, not sure whether he was angrier with her for arousing him or with himself for responding like a hormone-ridden adolescent. Calling on all his self-control, he made light conversation with the guide, whose name was John, while he adjusted his fins and rinsed his mask over the gunwale. Only then did he lower himself into the sea.

He let himself sink, as always struck by the myriad, sunshot hues of the sea. Favoring his ribs, he began to swim, the silky warmth of the water laving his body.

He needed a woman. That's what he needed. Just as long as her name wasn't Lia.

As he surfaced to breathe, he caught sight of her snorkel not that far ahead of him. He should head in the opposite direction, he thought, and knew he wasn't going to. Smoothly he took off in pursuit. When he was a few feet behind her, he sank again, watching her through the wavering currents of the tide. She was swimming steadily along the reef, her body lissome as a mermaid in her turquoise suit, her masked face giving her an alluring aura of mystery.

A turquoise suit. A mask.

Seth's eyes widened behind his own mask. His jaw dropped so that he inadvertently swallowed a mouthful of salt water. He surged to the surface, coughing and spluttering. He had to be wrong. His imagination was working overtime.

Lia d'Angeli his mysterious butterfly lover? Lia as the

woman at the ball in her shimmering turquoise bodysuit and her all-concealing mask?

He was out of his mind to even think it. Get a life, Seth. So you've never really forgotten her. So, subliminally, you know she ruined you for any other woman. So what?

You're letting a turquoise maillot and a snorkeling mask play tricks on you. Because you never really let her go.

He'd never admitted this to himself before. Seth cursed out loud. Which did he hate more, the fierce stab of hope that he'd found her again, or the swirling terror that he was wrong? He took a deep breath, filling his lungs, and again sank below the surface. The slow, graceful finning of her legs, the long arc of hip, waist and breast…had he ever forgotten them? Her face he'd never seen. But her body was unmistakable.

He should have recognized her the first moment he'd laid eyes on her in the foyer of the restaurant last night.

Again Seth rose to the surface, and this time conviction rose with him, hope replaced by certainty. The woman in Paris and the woman he'd met last night at the resort were one and the same. He'd found her. After eight years, he'd found her; and her name was Lia d'Angeli.

His first reaction was joy. Joy of a depth and intensity that was extraordinarily rare in his life.

But then, belatedly, Seth's brain started to work. Lia hadn't wanted to be found. She'd known his name from the beginning, and could have tracked him down anytime in the intervening years. Meeting him last night hadn't been her choice, he was sure of that. She'd been, to put it mildly, horrified and antagonistic. Not to mention enraged.

Why? What had he done? She was the one who'd disappeared. And he was damn well going to find out why.

He swam away from her, his movements choppy and uncoordinated. He felt as though he'd banged his head hard on the reef; or as though the bullet had hit a vital organ. But through the confusion of emotion in his chest he did know one thing. He wasn't going to have a shouting match with her while he was treading water within earshot of John the guide. No, the confrontation would keep. After eight years, another hour meant nothing.

Forty minutes later, Seth saw Lia heading for the dinghy. He got there first, trying to disguise how much it hurt to lever himself over the gunwales. When she reached the side of the boat, he held out his hand. "Let me help you," he said.

She yanked off her mask, throwing it over the gunwale, refusing to meet his eyes. The sunlight on her jaw…why had he taken so long to recognize her? It was all there. The slender line of her throat, the delicacy of her bones: he'd been an idiot not to have known who she was yesterday evening.

The instant he'd seen her, he'd lusted after her. That, too, had been a clue he'd ignored.

She said in a clipped voice, "I can manage."

"I'm sure you can. Grab my hand."

She could make a scene. Or she could do as he asked. With bad grace Lia took his hand, the strength in his fingers making her shiver with a mixture of panic and passionate longing. He lifted her as if she were weightless. When she'd gotten her footing in the boat, she tugged her hand free. "Thanks," she said grudgingly.

"No problem."

Scowling, she jammed her sunhat on her wet hair and threw the white shirt over her shoulders. She was going to need every one of the spa's ministrations to get rid of the tension that right now was tightening her muscles and seething along her nerves. Trying to gather her wits, she gave John the smile she hadn't given Seth, and said warmly, "That was wonderful, thanks so much for bringing us out here."

"You're welcome, ma'am."

He pulled the cord and the boat swirled in a circle to head

back to shore. The scene was like a picture postcard, from the tall palms to the white sand ruffled by waves. Her shirt flattened to her body, Lia gripped the thwart and knew that the minute the boat docked she was going to run for her cottage, go inside and lock the door.

As the dinghy nudged the dock, Seth uncoiled a rope and tied it to the bollard. Picking up his gear, he stepped out. Lia followed suit, clutching her fins to her chest like a shield as she said goodbye to John. She then started marching down the dock, the wood hot under her bare feet. Seth seized her by the elbow. "Slow down…we have to talk."

She whirled, trying to pull free. "We don't have to do anything—go away and leave me alone. Or I'll complain to the management."

He said flatly, "We're not going to have a fight in full view of the resort. You've got two choices. You can walk to your cottage and we'll talk there. Or I can pick you up and carry you."

"That kind of behavior went out with the Neanderthals… you're kind of slow to get the message."

His answer was to swing her up into his arms and stride off the dock straight for her cottage. He grated, "You have a reputation for privacy. So, as it happens, do I. Let's hope no one's watching us right now."

Years ago he'd picked her up and carried her out on a balcony where the lights of Paris had twinkled and shone. Fighting against memories whose potency had never really subsided, as well as the all-too-present potency of steel-strong arms and a taut, warm shoulder, Lia struck out at him with her elbow.

A flash of pure agony crossed his face. "Don't! I've got sore ribs."

"If you can't take the heat, don't go out in the sun," she snapped. She sure wasn't going to apologize; even though he was white about the mouth.

What had happened to his ribs?

What did she care?

He was marching toward her cottage, with its thick screen of bougainvillea and hibiscus. Too much privacy, Lia thought frantically. Privacy plus Seth Talbot equaled danger. "Put me down," she seethed, wriggling in his arms.

His hold tightened. "Where's your key?"

"If you think I'm letting you inside my cottage, you've got the wrong woman."

"No, I haven't." On impulse—because where in that skintight swimsuit could she possibly have hidden a key?—Seth tried her door, finding it unlocked. He shoved it open and plunked her down on the smoothly polished floor. "If it'll make you feel better, we'll leave the door wide-open. Okay, Lia d'Angeli, let's cut to the chase. I know who you are. You're the woman I went to bed with in Paris eight years ago—I've finally figured it out."

Rage almost choked her. "You've known all along who I was!"

"What the hell do you mean? You never gave me your name and you sneaked out in the middle of the night while I was asleep. For the better part of two weeks I had investigators turning over every cobblestone in Paris. Not a trace. You even used a false name when you rented your costume, for Pete's sake. You didn't want to be found—and now you accuse me of knowing who you were? Don't make me laugh."

He looked as far from laughter as a man could. "I used a false name because I wanted to be anonymous," she blazed. "I'd just won the two top European prizes, and the press was falling all over me—I wasn't just talented, I was also beautiful, sexy, voluptuous, you name it. They were having a field day and all I wanted to do was get away for a few hours. So, yes, I covered my tracks that night and I did leave in the middle of the night. But—"

"You could have gotten in touch with me later—or did that night mean so little to you?" He took her by the shoulders, his fingers digging into her flesh. "Forgettable sex—that's all it was for you?"

"I did!"

"Did what?" he snarled.

"I wrote you two letters," she said, biting off each word. "And now you dare pretend that you didn't get them?"

"When?"

Briefly she hesitated. His anger was so convincing, so powerful. What if there was a one in a million chance both letters had gone astray? What then? If she said two months later, wouldn't he twig to her pregnancy? Overriding all her other concerns was the certainty that she had to keep her beloved Marise out of the picture. "Not that long afterward," she said evasively and saw his eyes darken with suspicion.

"You're lying."

"I am not! I sent one to your headquarters in Manhattan, and the other to the Hamptons—I got the address off your Web site."

"That's my parents' place," Seth said, thinking furiously. "If you did write to me—and I'm far from convinced—what were the letters about?"

She said steadily, looking right at him, "I just wanted to stay in touch. That's all. But you never bothered answering. As we both know."

"It's pretty hard to answer a letter you never got," Seth said sarcastically.

"Why do you think I was so rude to you last night in the lobby? *Delighted to meet you,* you said. Then you had the gall to add, *I can't imagine how I've offended you.* As though we'd never made mad, passionate love for hours at a time in that ritzy hotel. It isn't me who's forgotten all that sex, it's you."

He pounced. "So you haven't forgotten?"

She bit her lip. As usual when she was in a temper, her

tongue was running away with her. "When you didn't do me the common courtesy of acknowledging my letters, I forgot about you in a hurry," she said, with absolutely no regard for the truth.

He said furiously, "One letter going astray I could understand. But two?"

"That's why I know you got them. Or, at the very least, one of them."

"So now you're accusing *me* of lying?"

"You're such a smart man," she said mockingly.

He thrust her away from him, prowling around the room. A yellow sweater was thrown over one of the bamboo chairs. A closed laptop computer rested on the teak table, while a music stand had been set up by the window with its magnificent view of the ocean. "How long are you staying?" he demanded.

Her nerves had tightened to an unbearable pitch. She'd left her bedroom door ajar; on the bureau was her favorite photo of Marise. Her daughter, and his. "I could ask you the same question."

"I leave in three days. What about you?"

"It's none of your business," she said coldly, keeping to herself the fact that she'd have only a day left of her holiday after he'd gone. "We have nothing to say to each other. You think I'm a liar, and I know you're one. Yes, we shared something many years ago. But it's over and done with and we've both moved on."

"Speak for yourself," he said softly, taking two swift steps toward her.

"Do you honestly think I could ever trust you again?" she cried. "I took the risk of getting in touch with you, and you chose to ignore me. Now you're paying the consequences. Grow up, Seth."

"Once I get home, I'm going to find out what happened to those two letters. Assuming you wrote them."

"It's too late to check your wastebasket."

His green eyes blazing with anger, Seth put his arms hard around her and dropped his mouth to hers in a kiss that was an impressive mix of rage and lust. Lia dug her fingers into his nape and kissed him back.

Fiercely she welcomed the first thrust of his tongue, greedy for more. Her hat tumbled to the floor. Her hands probed his damp hair, the taut line of his throat, the bump and curve of bone under his wet T-shirt, memory flooding her and casting aside caution.

Her response shot through Seth's body. He dragged the shirt from her shoulders, flinging it to the floor, then tugging the straps of her swimsuit down her arms. His mouth plummeted to find the sweet, bare curve of her breast. Her skin tasted of salt and sunlight, her nipple tight as coral. She gasped his name, throwing her head back, her heartbeat racing beneath his cheek.

He'd never wanted a woman as he wanted this one. And now he'd found her again.

She was yanking at the hem of his shirt, pressing her belly to his, her hips writhing. His arousal had been instant, fierce and imperative. He put one hand to her buttocks, jamming her against it, and kissed her again, tasting her, laving the slick heat of her mouth. Knowing he couldn't wait much longer, he lifted his head long enough to say hoarsely, "Let's go to the bedroom."

The bedroom…her photo of Marise.

She couldn't possibly allow Seth in her bedroom.

CHAPTER SEVEN

LIA went rigid in Seth's arms; he might as well have thrown a bucket of cold water in her face. "What's wrong with me?" she cried. "I'd have done it all over again—gone to bed with you and not a thought for—" She'd been about to say *the consequences*. In sheer panic she bit back the words. "Not a thought for tomorrow," she stumbled. "We don't know each other, we don't trust each other and yet we'd fall into bed?"

"You're the truest thing that's ever happened to me," Seth said harshly, and heard the words echo in his head. "Come to bed with me, Lia. Let me make love to you again. And this time I'll be able to see your face and call you by name…"

The intensity in his green eyes made her belly ache with longing. But she wasn't going to surrender to it. Or to him. How could she tell him about Marise when she couldn't condone his long silence? She said jaggedly, "Why didn't you answer my letters? Did you have another lover by then? Tell me, Seth. Tell me the truth! I swear I'll do my best to understand."

"Lia, I never got them," he said forcibly. "Do you think I wouldn't have answered? It took me nearly two years to replace you in my bed, and—hell, what am I saying? I've never been able to replace you, and that's the God's truth."

A truth he'd never intended sharing with anyone.

Lia gazed up at him. He was lying. He had to be. Two letters couldn't just disappear off the face of the earth. If only the stakes weren't so high, so impossibly weighted by the simple fact of Marise's existence. "Then what happened to them?" she demanded.

Ever since Lia had told him she'd sent one to the Hamptons, Seth had had his suspicions. But they were only suspicions, and a huge part of him dreaded for them to be proved true. He said flatly, "As soon as I get back to Manhattan, I'm going to find out. But I have to do it face-to-face."

"You're saying someone might have interfered with your personal mail? Someone at work? Or one of your parents? I can't believe that!"

His jaw an inflexible line, Seth said, "I don't want to talk about it until I have the facts."

"Well, I'm not going go to bed with you until I know. The letters are too important. Too basic."

He let out his breath in a frustrated sigh, moving away from her to pace up and down the room again. Like a caged tiger, she thought. She'd always hated zoos. Then he turned to face her. "You don't trust me."

"Of course I don't! Why should I?" His wet hair curled around his ears, his green eyes pinioning her like the butterfly she'd been. Stabbed with need, her whole body aching, Lia hugged her arms around her chest. "I'm cold," she said in a low voice. "You'd better go, Seth."

"So are we going to avoid each other for the next three days? Pretend we've never met?"

"If we're smart, that's exactly what we'll do."

Her head was downbent, and there were goosebumps on her bare arms. Stabbed with compunction—or that's what he chose to call it—Seth said impulsively, "Have dinner with me tonight, Lia. Just dinner." He added with a crooked smile, "We could call it a date. Seth meets Lia, they're attracted to each other, and he asks her out. You'll be quite safe—we won't make love on the floor of the Reef Room."

"I wouldn't bet on it, and the answer's no."

Seth came closer, deliberately running a finger down her cheek and watching her tiny shiver of response. "Eight o'clock in the Reef Room. In the meantime, have a hot shower… Lia, I'm sorry about the letters, more sorry than I can say. It must have hurt you when I didn't answer—typical guy, he has a one-night stand, gets what he wants and crosses you off the list. It was never that way, and I swear I'll find out who interfered with my mail."

Torn between the sincerity in his voice, and her own knowledge of just what it was she'd said in those letters, Lia struggled to find her bearings. Either he'd received at least one of her letters, in which case his sincerity was nothing but a ruthless ploy to get her in his bed again; or someone had destroyed both of them: a scenario she couldn't begin to encompass.

"I won't have dinner with you, Seth, it's playing with fire," she said evenly. "I don't trust a word you're saying—that's objection number one, and it's huge. There's more, though. Today was like a repeat of that masked ball—when I get within ten feet of you, I want to rip the clothes off your body and jump your bones. But I'm eight years older now, and I've learned a thing or two. No more one-night stands, for starters."

He opened his mouth to protest, and shut it again. Having found her for the second time, he'd been overwhelmed by his compulsive need to take her to bed again. But what then? He hadn't even thought about the consequences. If he went to bed with Lia in the warmth of a tropical island, could he walk away from her? Drop her, as sooner or later he dropped all his women?

Marriage was out, and he'd never wanted children. What did he have to offer but an affair? A six-week stand, he thought with a grimace.

She deserved better than that.

What was he going to do?

He said curtly, "Tomorrow then. Let's meet for breakfast. No risks attached."

"Your middle name is risk."

"So you've turned into a coward in the last eight years?"

"I'm being sensible," Lia cried. Wanting nothing more than to put her head down on the nearest pillow and weep her eyes out, she added, hearing the thread of desperation in her voice, "Please go."

"Nine o'clock tomorrow," Seth said in a steel voice. "The Reef Room. They do dynamite scrambled eggs."

"I hope you enjoy them. All by yourself."

"You'll turn up. I know you will. Because I've heard you play, and that woman doesn't know the meaning of cowardice or caution."

Two days ago, she would have agreed with him. Lia walked toward the door and pushed it wide, her fingers gripping the cool wood. The first thing she was going to do once he'd gone was hide the photo of Marise in the depths of her suitcase. She said with icy emphasis, "Stay away from me, Seth."

He brushed his lips against her cold cheek and heard himself say, "No…I'm too happy to have found you."

What did that have to do with a six-week stand?

For the second night in a row, Seth scarcely slept. This time, it wasn't nightmares that kept him awake. It was Lia.

Or rather, Lia's absence.

He hadn't laid eyes on her yesterday after he'd left her cottage. The knowledge that she was within a few hundred feet of him every minute of the day was a constant and powerful irritant. Unable to settle to anything, he went to bed at eleven, planning to make up for his lack of sleep the night before. But at 4:00 a.m. he was wide-awake and staring up into the darkness. It wasn't her absence that was the problem, no matter how empty his bed felt without her. It was her presence.

She wanted nothing to do with him. According to her, in those weeks after Paris she'd sent him two letters that he'd never bothered answering. A cold-blooded philanderer, that's how she saw him.

Had she really sent the letters?

If she hadn't, why would she bother constructing such an elaborate system of lies? And why would she be so angry with him?

Even if he left the letters out of the equation, this reunion was still horribly fraught. He had nothing to offer her. He'd never marry her; no amount of hot, glorious sex could change that.

But a one-night stand—or its equivalent—was also out. Lia d'Angeli wasn't like the women he always dated: emotionally cool, malleable, as rational in their way as he was in his. Lia was hot-tempered, strong-willed, intense and generous. All he had to do was think back eight years to know just how generous.

He couldn't mess around with her. One of her strengths as a musician was that she took risks, opening herself to the music and making herself vulnerable. She'd do the same in bed with him, he knew it. He couldn't abuse that vulnerability, any more than he could take advantage of her generosity.

Several months ago, a friend in Berlin had introduced him to one of her CDs. He'd never forget how her playing had penetrated every one of his defenses; it was as though she knew him intimately, and was addressing only himself: the lonely little boy he'd been, the guarded man he'd become.

After that, he'd bought every one of her recordings. But he'd never gone to a live recital. He'd known it would be too much for him; he loathed exposing his emotions in public.

So he'd never seen her in the flesh. He always steered away from reading reviews of music, preferring to make up his own mind, and the society pages weren't part of his reading matter; he also, therefore, knew very little about her. But there was one more reason he hadn't recognized her in the lobby of the Tradewind Room. Her CDs all had reproductions of famous paintings on the cover; her own photo, if there at all, was tucked somewhere in the liner notes, her face merged with those of the players in the orchestra. Presumably it had been against her principles to use her beauty as a sales pitch.

Hadn't she refused to have dinner with him last night because of her principles? She didn't trust him, and therefore was refusing point blank to spend time with him. Odds were he'd be eating breakfast alone.

If that's what happened, he'd track her down afterward and tell her calmly and logically that she was right, they shouldn't see each other again; it was out of the question that he have either a brief fling with her, or commit to any kind of longstanding relationship. He'd keep the whole thing low-key and under control.

Game over. Before it had begun.

As for himself, there'd be no risk that, once again, she'd touch him in that indefinable place called the soul. It had taken too long to get over her the last time. He didn't want a repeat.

His decision made, Seth should have found it easy to fall asleep. The numbers on the clock jumped from one digit to the next; the night sky slowly lightened, and the birds began warming up outside his window in a medley of chortles, whistles and screams.

It didn't matter what his decision was, Seth thought in near despair. He still wanted Lia. If she were here with him now, her slender warm body pressed to his, he'd be kissing her until he couldn't breathe, tasting her skin, exploring its every secret…dammit, why couldn't the birds shut up?

At six Seth got out of bed, dragged a T-shirt over his head

and went outside. He had three hours before he met Lia for breakfast. He lay down in the hammock strung between two tall trees, wedging a pillow under his head. The sky was a gentle eggshell blue, washed with streaks of pale pink and gold. Listening to the soft shushing of waves on the sand, he closed his eyes. He wouldn't sleep. But at least it would be better than being caged up indoors…

In the dream, it was blinding sunlight. Mud huts, an army jeep, a mute array of helpless villagers. The soldiers were dragging a mother away from her little boy. The boy was screaming. As one of the soldiers took out his machete, Seth gave a hoarse shout of horror and ran toward him. But his feet were as heavy as lead and he couldn't cover the ground quick enough. The machete was descending and again he shouted…

"Seth! Wake up, please wake up!"

He was tangled in ropes, his whole body bathed in sweat. Seth's eyes flew open. Lia was bending over him, shaking him by the shoulder, her dark eyes appalled. The sun made a brilliant aureole behind her head.

He wasn't in Africa. He was at the White Cay Resort. Tangled up in a hammock. The machete still inscribing its deadly arc in his mind, Seth rasped, "What the hell are you doing here?"

"I was walking back to breakfast when I heard you yell— I thought someone was murdering you."

His humiliation that she'd heard him screeching like a banshee translated itself into rage. Seth yanked his fingers free from the weave of the hammock and swung his feet to the ground. "Just what were you going to do if someone was?"

"I don't know—I hadn't got that far. Were you having a nightmare?"

He stood up, swaying momentarily. As she grabbed for his arm, he shook her hand off, his face a rictus of fury. "Why don't you get lost?"

"I asked you a question."

"Which I'm choosing not to answer."

Her lashes flickered. "You're ashamed of yourself," she said pithily. "Embarrassed. Because I've seen a part of you that's private."

"Whadda ya know," he snarled, "you're not just gorgeous, you've got brains as well. Vamoose, Lia."

It would have been all too easy to have snarled back. Lia had had very little sleep, and what she'd managed to get had been riddled with dreams so sexually explicit that she'd been more than embarrassed. The object of those dreams was now glaring at her, all six feet three of him. But when she'd woken Seth a couple of minutes ago, the sick horror in his eyes had struck her to the heart. Horror, pain and helplessness…they'd all been there. Reining in her errant temper, she said tightly, "Let me tell you something about myself. My father was Italian, a very famous baritone—"

"Arturo d'Angeli," Seth interrupted impatiently. "I'm not a total ignoramus." His voice gentled. "I read somewhere that he and your mother were both killed in a car crash several years ago."

"When I was eighteen. I still miss them." Grimacing, Lia picked up her train of thought. "My father was passionate and romantic, all his emotions as volatile as an erupting volcano— including his rages, which were legendary. My mother was Norwegian, though. A harpsichordist of world renown, who was cool, rational and controlled."

"Gudrun Halvardson."

"Right now I'm trying very hard not to act like my father. To be my mother instead. Calm and moderate." Lia's voice rose. "Even though I'd like to bang your head on the nearest tree."

Despite himself, a smile tugged at Seth's lips. A reluctant smile, maybe. But still a smile. "I hate to tell you—Arturo's winning."

"Why wouldn't he? You're so goldarn stubborn! Stubborn,

strong and silent. A bad combo—in my books, that adds up to dull. Deadly dull. So why don't you tell me what you were dreaming about?"

Her hair, black as a raven's wing, had the same blue glint of raven feathers in the sun. She was wearing a dress he hadn't seen before, the fabric a dizzying swirl of red, black and white. Her earrings were huge red hoops, while clunky red and white enamel bracelets circled her wrists. "You won't get lost in a crowd," he said.

"If that's supposed to be a compliment, I'm underwhelmed."

Before he could lose his nerve, Seth said rapidly, "I was in central Africa last week. Saw more than I wanted to of a local insurrection—that's what I was dreaming about. If you'll give me five minutes, I'll shower and take you to breakfast."

Her face softened. She said quietly, "I was part of a benefit concert to raise money for AIDS's relief in Africa last year. I made myself look at a lot of news footage…I had awful dreams for weeks afterward. I can't imagine what it would be like to actually see that kind of stuff."

He ran his fingers through his hair. "It's the kids that get to me. I can't get them out of my mind."

"Why were you there? On business?"

He could have lied; he rarely talked about this side of his personality. "I started a charitable foundation several years ago…it's grown over the years, perhaps you've heard of it."

She shook her head. "After you didn't answer my letters, I avoided any mention of you in the press."

He labored on. "I take a personal interest in it—visit all the places to see the money goes to make people as independent as possible."

Her brow wrinkled. "Not just handouts, you mean."

"Right."

Lia gazed at him thoughtfully. There was a lot he wasn't saying, but she was quite capable of filling in the gaps. He was involved. He cared. And in the process, he put his life on the line. "Yesterday, when you kissed me in my cottage, I noticed there was a bandage around your ribs."

He winced. "Bullets were flying. I didn't duck fast enough."

Lia picked a leaf from the nearest shrub, absently rubbing it between her fingers. He was a man of integrity, that's what she'd learned in the last few minutes. How could she square that with the man who hadn't answered her letters? *It's the kids that get to me,* that's what he'd just said. So would he have disregarded any responsibility toward his own child?

As if this would give her the answers she sought, she stepped forward, looped her arms around his waist and reached up to kiss him, her breasts pressed to the hardness of his chest.

Seth went utterly still. Then he pulled his head back. "Don't, Lia," he said.

She quivered as though he'd struck her. "Why not?"

"I figured something out in the night—I was going to tell you at breakfast."

"You'd better tell me now."

She'd moved back from him, her dark eyes wary. Get it over with, Seth, he thought. The quicker the better. "For reasons of my own, I'm not into marriage and I don't want children. You're not the kind of woman I can have a casual affair with—on one day, off the next. That didn't work eight years ago, and I see no reason why it would work now." He gave her a faint smile. "I should have listened to you yesterday when you told me to leave you alone—because you were right."

I don't want children... Clenching her fists, she pushed the words away and said sharply, "You're not in love with me?"

"Of course not. Nor was I eight years ago. But whatever happened between us meant something to me."

"Why are you so opposed to marriage and having a family? They're normal enough needs."

His face closed against her. "It's a long story, and not one I'm about to tell."

Her brain made another lightning-swift leap. "I sent one of my letters to your parents' house—if I can believe you when you say you didn't get them, then it's possible they're the ones who intercepted the letters. Do they hate you? Is that what the problem is?"

"Lay off," he said in an ugly voice.

"Don't tell me what to do! Was it your parents who scared you off commitment? How, Seth?"

He said with vicious emphasis, "Thick-skinned doesn't begin to describe you—you've got a hide like a rhinoceros."

"It'd take a rhinoceros to make any impression on you." Or a rebel bullet, she thought sickly. "I hate this conversation," she muttered. "Surely we don't have to stand here trading insults like a couple of kids."

He said brusquely, "I'll leave here a day early, and in the meantime I'll make sure our paths don't cross."

"So you can be hostage to your parents for the rest of your life?" she cried, and wondered if, deep down, she wasn't fighting for Marise as much as for herself.

"You have no right to ask questions like that."

She had every right. Because Marise, particularly since she'd started school and met other children, all of whom had fathers, had on occasion expressed the wish that her own father appear on the scene. A wish that Lia had been quite unable to fulfill.

Marise's father was standing right in front of her. Adamant, hostile and immovable. She said, not bothering to mask the bitterness in her voice, "Very well. I'll eat in the Tradewind Room and I'll do my best to stay out of your way. Goodbye, Seth. Have a comfortable life."

He made no move to stop her as she turned on her heel and left the clearing behind his cottage. His face had been like a mask, she thought. Hard and empty, blank-eyed.

She'd totally lost her appetite. Lia hurried back to her cottage and went inside. It looked exactly as it had when she'd left. It was herself who'd changed.

The only man she'd slept with in eight years wouldn't so much as kiss her. Wouldn't marry her, or have an affair with her. Certainly would never act as a father to their child.

And how that hurt.

When Marise had first asked about her father, Lia had said carefully, "We only met once, Marise. He wasn't able to marry me, and we've never been in touch."

"Was he nice?" four-year-old Marise had asked, big-eyed.

"Very nice."

"Can we go for ice cream now?"

So the two of them had walked down the lane from the old farmhouse to the little village, where they'd eaten banana splits in the shadows of the tall elms…

So long ago, Lia thought with a sigh. She'd have to keep this meeting with Seth a secret. How could she possibly tell Marise that the man who'd fathered her didn't want to have children?

Tension was knotting her shoulders again, just as if she hadn't spent a wad of money yesterday at the spa. She could do with a massage right now, Lia thought, opening her laptop to check her e-mails. There was one from Nancy, with a digital photo of Marise grinning at the camera in her long white nightgown, her brown hair tumbling down her back. In a surge of love and protectiveness Lia gazed at the image, into eyes the green of summer meadows. The farm that was their home was called, appropriately, Meadowland.

Should she tell Seth he was a father? When she'd mailed the two letters, that had been her decision: he had the right to know. Maybe, just maybe, he hadn't gotten those letters. But did that change anything? Marise wasn't an unborn baby anymore; she was seven years old, trusting and vulnerable.

In all this mess, one thing was clear. Marise mustn't get hurt.

Added to that, Seth didn't want any further involvement with Lia herself: he'd made that clear a few minutes ago. Not that he'd ever really been involved with her. So why did she feel like bawling her head off? Just like Marise when she fell down, or when one of her friends was mean to her.

Damned if she was going to cry her eyes out over a man who was all over her one day and then the next wouldn't even kiss her. Lia peeled and ate a mango, scarcely tasting the juicy yellow flesh, then changed into her swimsuit. However, a very vigorous swim in the sea didn't help at all. She was tired, she was hungry, and her brain was in a state of total confusion. Moral dilemmas were just that: dilemmas. Difficult to solve, and without any assurance that the choice made was the right one. Should she or shouldn't she tell Seth about Marise?

Sooner or later, he'd read something about her daughter. Although Lia did her best to keep Marise safe from any publicity, the media had a long reach and an even longer memory. Wouldn't it be better to tell him herself rather than have him find out by accident?

She didn't know. She simply didn't know. Maybe telling him was no big deal: if he didn't want children, he'd pay no more attention to Marise now than he had since her conception.

Lia gritted her teeth. She'd despise Seth if he neglected her daughter that way.

After showering the salt from her hair and skin, Lia dressed in shorts and a brief top, and took her precious Stradivarius violin from its case. The truths of music had always sustained her in times of trouble; perhaps they'd help her now. She tuned the violin and began to play, standing by the window of her bedroom with its view of jade-green sea and gently swaying palm trees.

She should practice the Brahms she'd be playing in Vienna next week. Instead she let her mind wander, drifting from melody to melody, pouring into the music all her confusion and pain.

How could one man have so much power over her?

CHAPTER EIGHT

SETH had gone to the Reef Room for breakfast, burying his nose in the newspaper and eating the food as if it was so much sawdust. He'd done the right thing by ousting Lia from his life. So why did he feel like a number-one louse?

He rattled the papers irritably, trying to concentrate on the latest uprising in the Philippines. But Lia's face kept intruding itself between him and the newsprint. She'd fought, but she hadn't begged. She'd been hurt, but she hadn't cried.

He wanted her as he'd wanted no other woman in his life. Was she right? Was he still in thrall to his parents? One thing he knew: when he got home, he was driving straight to the huge stone mansion where he'd grown up and confronting his mother about the letters. His father would never have tampered with Seth's mail; but Eleonore could have, Seth thought, sickened. She'd have seen Lia as a penniless musician after the Talbot money; but did that mean she'd behaved so underhandedly? So maliciously?

He wanted answers from her, and he was going to get them.

Were the kids he got so involved with through the foundation his surrogate children? Had a woman ever shaken him up as Lia could?

With a low growl of frustration Seth folded the paper and

left the restaurant. He was going to bury himself in work today and forget about Lia d'Angeli.

But as he sat down in front of his computer, through the open window drifted, faintly, the notes of a violin. She was playing, he thought. Three cottages away, the wind carrying the music toward him. Slowly he got up, the melody tugging him like a magnet.

He threaded his way through the lush gardens behind the cottages, the sun hot on his shoulders. When he got to Lia's cottage, he walked around to the front and stood still for a few minutes on the steps, listening intently, feeling all her unhappiness and uncertainty as his own. But as each perfect note took possession of him, the last of Seth's doubts vanished. Lia had written the letters: her music searched too profoundly for truth for him to doubt her word.

His mind shied away from the mechanics of their disappearance. Later, he thought. Later.

That she'd written to him must mean she'd longed to reconnect with him. No wonder she'd been so hurt and angry when they'd met again, here on the island.

He had to tell her he believed her.

The front door was unlocked. Seth pushed it open and walked in. Her laptop was on the table, open, the screensaver shifting brightly colored musical notes from top to bottom and side to side. She must be in the bedroom; she'd shifted from Tchaikovsky's lyricism to a modernistic lament, full of dissonance and a wild, unappeasable grief. Struck to the heart, his feet anchored to the floor, Seth forgot this wasn't his cottage or his computer; with his mind on automatic pilot, his fingers briefly hit the space bar.

An image flashed onto the screen, distracting him from the music. A little girl wearing a white nightgown was smiling right at him. A very pretty little girl with brown curly hair and green eyes.

Green like his.

Seth sank down into the nearest chair, his gaze riveted to the screen. The little girl's chin was tilted, just as Lia sometimes tilted hers. Lia's child, he thought numbly. She looked to be about seven.

His child?

He'd used no protection that night in the hotel in Paris. It could be his child. Was that why Lia had written him two letters, two so that he'd get the news even if one of them by chance went astray?

How often did he see eyes of a true, deep green? It had to be his child.

He, Seth, was the father of a daughter.

His heart was thudding in his chest as though he'd run from one end of the island to the other. His hands were ice-cold. For over seven years he'd been a father, and hadn't known it. Seven long years...

As he pushed back the chair, it scraped on the floor. The music stopped with startling abruptness. From the bedroom Lia called, "Is someone there?"

His voice was stuck somewhere in his throat. He heard her footsteps pad across the polished wood floor and from a long way away watched her walk into the living room. She was still holding her bow and violin. When she saw him, she stopped dead in her tracks.

Seth, Lia thought. In her cottage. In front of her laptop with its photo of Marise. He was white-faced, his eyes blank with shock. She took a deep breath and said, trying hard to be calm and instead sounding heartless, "She's your child, Seth."

He cleared his throat. "I'd already figured that out."

"That's why I wrote to you, two months after we met. To tell you I was pregnant. But you say you didn't get my letters."

"I didn't—although I do believe you wrote them. Whoever

intercepted them has a lot to answer for," he said, his voice as clipped as a robot's. "What's her name?"

"Marise. She's seven."

"Does she know about me?"

"Not really…when she first asked about you, I told her I'd known you only very briefly, and that you couldn't marry me. She's never asked your name."

He said with painful truth, "You were left alone to bear my child. I've never seen her, written to her, given you any money for her support—"

"I didn't write to you because I wanted money!"

"I never said you did." He asked another crucial question. "Why didn't you tell me about her yesterday?"

"How could I, when I still don't know what to believe about the letters? For someone to have intercepted them—intervened in your life and mine so callously—it's monstrous."

"Yes," Seth said quietly, "it was monstrous."

"Plus you were so intent on informing me you didn't want children. Never had and, I presumed, never would. What was I supposed to do?"

"Were you planning to tell me at some time in the future?"

"I don't know." She put the violin and bow down on the table, running her fingers through the silky darkness of her hair. "That's why I was playing. To try to figure out what I was going to do."

Some of his anger escaped in spite of himself. "You should have told me the minute we met!"

"When I was introduced to you in the lobby? *Oh hi, Seth, nice to see you again—what's it been? Eight years? By the way, I left your daughter home this trip.* Give me a break."

"You've been acting ever since we met. Lying to me, in effect." Wasn't that what really hurt?

"It's not that simple," she fumed. "I won't risk hurting my daughter, Seth. Not if you're going to pull another vanishing

that's no problem. But you have a child, a real live flesh-and-blood child. Fatherhood requires commitment—it sounds to me like you're commitment-phobic."

He was. Always had been. "I can't ignore Marise, as though she doesn't exist. I've been landed with a commitment, like it or not. Just as you were left pregnant, like it or not." He scowled at her. "What have you got against marriage?"

She scowled right back, pulling free from the circle of his arm. "I don't have the time for it."

"You're too busy being a musician and a single mother."

"Exactly."

"If you were married, you wouldn't be a single mother."

"If you're so clever, will you kindly explain to me how we're going to handle this?" she exploded. "What about us? We just have to look at each other and our hormones spike way off the chart. Marise is trusting and innocent. I won't carry on an affair right under her nose."

"That's right, you won't. I'll visit her when you're not there."

Trying desperately to conceal how his casual dismissal had hurt her, Lia said, "Don't you get it? We'll be tied together for years."

"We'll both be free to live our own lives."

She gripped the edge of the table. "We first saw each other, masked and costumed, across a crowded ballroom. But we recognized each other right away. We're playing with fire here, Seth."

"Marise exists. I have to see her."

Feeling utterly exhausted, Lia leaned back on the table. If Seth were to meet Marise, it would be at Meadowland. Which was Lia's sanctuary, her home, the place where love bloomed, unforced and peaceful as the wildflowers of the meadows. How could she bear for Seth to invade it?

He said inflexibly, "Let's set a date right now—have you

got your datebook handy?" Because he'd been working, his Palm Pilot was in his pocket. He took it out. "How about one day next week?"

She said in a hostile voice, "I'm playing in Vienna with Ivor Rosnikov a week from today."

Rosnikov was a wildly popular Russian pianist with a well-earned reputation as a womanizer. The words were out before Seth could censor them. "Is he your current lover?"

"If he is, that's none of your business. Didn't you just say I was free to live my own life?"

He had. Not one of his smarter pronouncements. "He's bedded half the women in Europe."

"He's also a marvelous musician," she snapped.

There was a red smudge under her chin where her violin had rested. Seth stared at it, willing himself to stay where he was. But a split second later, he was crushing her to his chest, kissing her as though she was the only woman in the world. All the curves of her body, the sweetness of her mouth, were so achingly familiar, so passionately desired...

Lia clung to him, her lips parted to the dance of his tongue, her hips tight to the surge of his arousal; and knew she'd come home. Home? she thought in confusion. Meadowland is home. Not Seth. Seth's too dangerous, too unpredictable.

Then he thrust her away, his breathing harsh in his ears. "You can kiss me like that, and tell me in the same breath you're Rosnikov's lover?"

"I never said I was!"

Sunlight was flickering through her hair like tiny electric sparks. Seth said implacably, "Tell me when I can meet Marise."

"I'll decide whether you can or not after you've found out about the letters. After you've had time to think very hard about what fatherhood implies. Marise has done just fine without a father for seven years. I won't allow you to wander in and out of her life as your busy schedule permits—I won't have her hurt, Seth."

"I'm damned if you'll deprive her of her father!"

"I'll give you my phone numbers, including my cell. You can get in touch with me after Vienna. Assuming you can offer me concrete proof about the letters, we'll talk then."

He said, keeping any trace of emotion from his voice, "I know you sent them. I believe you, in other words. I trust you. Why can't you do the same for me?"

"Try seeing it from my point of view," she flared. "Eight years ago I was convinced you'd abandoned me, betraying our lovemaking in Paris by ignoring its consequences. The hurt went deep. Much too deep for me to now say blithely, *sure, we'll sleep together, Seth, and of course you can see my daughter any time that's convenient for you.*"

"It wasn't my fault that you were abandoned. Nor will I be kept from Marise."

"But you'd have to make a genuine commitment to her—I'm not sure you're capable of that."

She looked as fierce as a mother bear defending her cub. Deep within him, respect stirred, mixed with unwilling admiration. He spoke the simple truth. "The commitment's already made. The moment I saw Marise's green eyes, I had no choice."

Lia let out her breath in a long sigh. "I play again with Ivor in Hamburg two days after Vienna. Then I fly home." She did some quick calculations. "The fifteenth. You can call me then."

He already knew he wasn't going to wait that long: a piece of information he kept to himself. If Lia d'Angeli thought she was going to call all the shots, she'd very soon find out she was wrong. "Fine," Seth said.

She'd expected him to argue. Conscious of a huge sense of anticlimax, Lia said, "When are you leaving the island?"

"Tomorrow morning."

"I'll get room service the rest of the day."

I'll stay out of your way—that's what she meant. And wasn't that what he wanted, too? He took a scrap of paper from his pocket and wrote down the number for his personal cell phone, along with his e-mail address. "Will you forward me that photo of Marise?"

Briefly she closed her eyes. "Yes."

"Thanks." What else was there to say? Or do? He sure wasn't going to kiss her again.

There were faint blue shadows under her eyes and a tired droop to her mouth. He said roughly, "Take care of yourself, Lia," and let himself out the door.

His personal jet couldn't get here until tomorrow. Otherwise he'd be leaving right now. Getting as far away from Lia as he could.

Lia d'Angeli, the mother of his child.

Dawn was normally Lia's favorite time of the day: everything fresh, the illusion of a new beginning, the flourish of hope as the sun broke the horizon.

On this, Seth's last morning on the island, she merely felt miserably unhappy. After he'd left her cottage yesterday, she'd practiced her heart out, until she was more confident of the Brahms *cadenza*. She'd eaten outside on the patio, trying to convince herself she was getting the solitude and peace she craved. She'd even slept, off and on.

There was no reason to feel so jangled and off-center. She'd kept in control of the situation yesterday, insisting Seth meet her terms. Well, almost in control. That kiss didn't exactly qualify; and was no doubt the reason she'd woken so early this morning.

When she got up, Lia had decided a swim might settle her nerves. Now she lay back in the saltwater, trying to empty her mind of anything but the beauty of her surroundings. On the waves, pearl-pink flecks reflected the dawn sky; a white tropic bird winged overhead, its long streamers flashing in the light. The sand was newly washed, the tulip tree near her cottage blazoned with huge orange blooms, each a miniature sunrise.

She'd feel a lot better once she knew Seth had left.

Hold that thought, Lia.

She was trying to as, fifteen minutes later, she wandered up the beach toward her cottage, tugging off her swimcap and shaking out her long black hair. On the boardwalk, she used the little tap to rinse the sand from her feet, absently admiring the iridescent polish on her toenails. Frosted Mocha. She must buy it again.

In the bushes, a bird gave a loud squawk of alarm. Lia glanced up, every nerve on alert. Her pulse skipped a beat. Seth had just emerged onto the beach, wearing skintight navy trunks, a towel slung over his shoulder. He hadn't seen her.

Then, as though he sensed her watching him, he looked right at her. The sun was in his eyes. He raised one hand, shading his face, and started walking toward her.

Her heart was pounding in her rib cage; her feet were glued to the boardwalk. As he came closer, she saw that he'd removed the tape that had circled his chest. The scar, a livid, angry red, traversed his ribs from front to back.

He could have been killed, she thought. If the bullet had gone a mere two inches to the left, she would never have seen him again. Did anything matter beside the immensity of that fact? Calmly, as though it was what she'd intended all along, Lia walked to meet him.

To Seth, she looked like a goddess from the sea in her wet turquoise suit, the sunlight glinting on the droplets of water on her skin. Her level gaze was confident of its power, her gait so graceful it hurt him somewhere deep inside, a place he only rarely allowed to be touched. He swallowed hard, knowing he should run in the opposite direction, knowing equally strongly he was going to do nothing of the sort.

She was his fate.

He didn't believe in fate.

Then she reached him. With that same confidence she looped her arms around his neck, stood on tiptoes and kissed him full on the mouth.

Desire slammed through him, hot and powerful. The kiss deepened, until Seth was aware of nothing but a fury of need. Her breasts, pressed to his bare chest, were hard-tipped, her nipples like tiny shells; grasping her by the hips, he ground her body to his, swamped by wave after wave of desire.

Not here, he thought, desperately reaching for some restraint, you can't make love to Lia on the beach. He took her by the hand, rubbing his cheek against the silky fragrance of her hair, and tried to slow his breathing. "Let's go to my cottage," he said huskily, and watched her smile her assent.

Hand in hand, they walked the length of the boardwalk toward his cottage. Ushering her in, Seth kicked the door shut behind him and led her to his bedroom. He hadn't made the bed, Lia noticed; the tumbled sheets where he'd spent the night seemed incredibly intimate to her. Turning to face him, she said urgently, "I want to make love to you again, Seth. I want to stand naked in front of you."

As she strained upward, his head dropped to find her mouth; her lips were salty, soft and warm and passionately hungry. She drew his hips to hers, her fingers probing his taut buttocks. He said hoarsely, "You drive me crazy, Lia. But this time we mustn't forget—"

Quickly he opened the drawer on the bedside table, and took out a small foil envelope. She said in an odd voice, "Would I have thought of that?"

"Just as long as one of us remembers." His voice deepened. "I want you so much…"

"You can have me. All of me. Now."

Reaching up, he dragged the turquoise straps off her shoulders. Her breasts were fuller than he remembered, their tips a rosy-pink in the dawn light. He slid the wet fabric down her hips, kneeling to pull the suit all the way to her slender, high-arched feet. Then he buried his face in her belly, moving lower, his hands clasping her thighs.

She opened to him, burying her fingers in his thick blond hair, throwing back her head in ecstasy as he parted the petals of her flesh and unerringly found her center. Like wildfire, the climax ripped through her, so powerful that she cried out in mingled shock and satiation.

Slowly Seth rose to his feet, his mouth traveling all the curves of her body until he was standing upright. She said, trying to catch her breath, "Do you know what? I want more—how can I? It's disgraceful!"

"We've scarcely begun," he said, his eyes trained on her face as she pulled back from him, her smile infinitely seductive. She was tugging at his chest hair, sliding her fingers over the rippled muscles of his belly, then edging his swimsuit free of his erection. The brush of her fingers against his taut flesh nearly drove him over the brink. As he kicked the suit to the floor, she said, "Your body's so beautiful…kiss me, Seth—now. Drive me out of my mind."

It was all he needed to hear. Devouring the delectable softness of her lips, his teeth grazing her tongue, he drank deep of all the sweetness that was Lia. She was so willing, so eager, so incredibly generous that within moments he lost the last shred of his control. Flinging her back on the bed, he cupped her breast and took her nipple into his mouth, suckling her as she whimpered his name. Briefly he raised his head, drinking in the stunned pleasure on her face; her rib cage was a long arch, her eyes dark pools in which he could lose himself. You're mine, he thought. All mine.

Her hands were everywhere, teasing and enticing until they encircled him in a paradoxical mixture of passion and gentleness. Wasn't that the essence of Lia, Seth thought in sudden insight; and then stopped thinking altogether. "I can't wait," he gasped, shoving himself up on his elbows and reaching for the envelope. He dealt with it swiftly, even as her legs widened to gather him in.

As he plunged deep, her face convulsed, her breath rasping in her throat. Like a great surge of the sea, he was lifted until he could no longer withstand her fierce inner throbbing; they fused and fell together in a tumble of dazzling whiteness.

Joined, Seth rolled on his side, pulling her with him. He dropped his face to her shoulder, dimly aware that his forehead was filmed with sweat. Salty, he thought. Like the sea.

Her heart was thrumming, her body limp. He muttered, "Lia, are you okay?"

His voice seemed to come from miles away. Slowly Lia came back to herself, to the weight of Seth's arm over her ribcage and the hammerbeat of his heart so close it echoed in her ears. So close it could have been her own.

But it wasn't her own. It was Seth's. Seth, with whom she'd just made love.

It had happened again. Just like in Paris.

What had she said to him yesterday? *I won't have an affair with you.*

This high-minded stance had lasted less than twenty-four hours. The basic truth was that she couldn't keep her hands off him. Not here on a tropical island. Not, in all likelihood, at Meadowland, were he to go there. Meadowland, where Marise lived.

"Are you all right, Lia?" Seth repeated patiently.

"No."

She'd burrowed her head deeper into the pillow, hiding

from him. Seth pulled free of her, went to the bathroom, then marched back into the bedroom; she was lying in exactly the same pose.

His heart now felt cold in his chest. Making love to Lia definitely hadn't been in his plans. Or in hers, he'd be willing to bet. In spite of himself, he glanced over at the clock. His plane was due to take off in less than two hours.

He knelt on the bed and tugged on the silken fall of her hair. "Look at me."

She reared up, her dark eyes hostile. "We're like a couple of alley cats—we can't keep doing this!"

"It's only the second time in eight years."

"We've only seen each other twice in eight years," she flashed with impeccable logic. "You can't meet Marise—I won't allow it. I won't have her hurt because you and I behave like sex maniacs."

"Listen to me, Lia," Seth said forcefully, and wondered who he was trying to convince, himself or her. "All the trappings of romance were in place this morning—tropical beach at dawn, you in that goddamned swimsuit, wet from the sea—what did you expect? Your farm won't be like that—it's domesticated, a family setting, you even have a nanny, for Pete's sake. I've steered clear of stuff like that for years. A total turnoff."

"If you're going to have anything to do with Marise, you're going to tell me why the mere thought of a nanny makes you go into orbit."

"I'll tell you what I choose to tell you, and no more."

She hated it when his eyes went as hard and sharp-edged as emeralds. "I call the shots as far as Marise is concerned," she announced with matching adamancy, and in a flurry of bare limbs rolled off the bed and grabbed for her swimsuit. It was cold and damp, gritty with sand. She yanked it up her body, wishing with all her heart she'd gone to any other island than this one for her yearly vacation.

Seth stood up, seizing her by the elbow. "I'll be in touch after your concerts and we'll make the arrangements then."

"No, Seth," she said softly, "first you'll find out what happened to my letters and you'll tell me about it. The how and the why."

"Twenty minutes of scorching sex sure hasn't affected your brain."

"I'm fighting for two—not just for myself."

With no idea where the words came from, Seth said, "What if I'm fighting for three?"

"You're not. So don't kid yourself."

She was right. He wasn't. "I've always dated malleable women who never raise their voices," he said caustically. "No danger of that with you."

"None whatsoever."

"Say it, Lia. Before you're the one who goes into orbit."

"A nice faraway orbit sounds like a fabulous idea. You can get in touch with me once I'm home from my concerts and I wish to heaven you'd put some clothes on."

Her eyes were dark pools of fury. He stepped closer. "We could shower together before you leave—that way we save water."

"Conservation's a very fine cause, but it's not my top priority right now."

"What is your top priority, darling Lia?"

If his eyes had been jewel-hard a few moments ago, they now held all the shifting greens of a tropical sea. "Darling Seth," she retorted, "it's to get out of here so I don't spend the rest of the day ravaging your body."

He lowered his head and kissed her with lazy sensuality. Then, taking his time, he nibbled his way along her lower lip, seeing with considerable satisfaction how her eyes were now blurred with desire. For once, he wasn't going to yield to that desire. He'd show her—and himself—that he could resist her.

"We both have to get out of here," he said agreeably. "I have a business to run and you have to practice. I'll see you in a week or so." Then he stepped back, hoping she couldn't hear the pounding of blood in his veins.

She was gaping at him, looking totally at a loss. He added kindly, "Shut your mouth, sweetheart, you look like a stranded fish. Enjoy the rest of your stay, won't you?"

She snapped, "I will. Without you. Dearest."

Then she whirled and stalked out the door, slamming it hard behind her. Seth winced at the noise and sank down on the bed. The empty bed. Which was rumpled, and smelled sweetly of Lia.

He should have canceled his jet. What was the use of being the boss if he couldn't do as he pleased?

He wasn't the boss where Lia was concerned. His glands were. Brute testosterone. Him and Australopithecus.

He loved the way she never gave an inch.

Loved it? What kind of language was that?

CHAPTER NINE

SETH marched up the steps, ignoring the stone lions at their base. The whole house—or, more accurately, the whole mansion—was made of stone. Like his mother's heart, he thought grimly, and let himself in with his key. He'd phoned Eleonore to let her know he was coming; he hadn't seen either of his parents for several months.

The entrance hall with its marble floor and enormous arched windows was intended to intimidate; the architecture as well as the rigidly formal gardens were, in his opinion, totally mismatched to their surroundings of ocean and woods. Surroundings that had allowed him the escape he'd needed as a little boy.

He took the wide oak stairs two at a time, loosening his tie as he went. He hadn't planned what he was going to say. He scarcely needed to.

Tapping on the door of his mother's private sitting room, he walked in without waiting for her to answer. Heavy velvet drapes and carved mahogany furniture fought against the light coming through the tall windows. Fought and won, Seth thought. "Hello, Mother," he said.

He dropped a dutiful kiss on her cheek. Every one of her iron-gray hairs was in place, her black Valentino suit was elegant without ostentation, and diamonds sparkled on her fingers. She said coolly, "Your tie's a disgrace."

He hauled it over his head and threw off his jacket; Eleonore always kept the room too warm for his taste. "I just flew in from the Caribbean."

"Would you like tea? A drink?"

"No. This isn't a social call." He paused for a moment, wishing, as he'd always wished, that he could see even a sliver of warmth in her cold blue eyes.

"Then why don't you come to the point?" she said.

"Eight years ago, in Paris, I had a brief affair with a woman whose name I never knew," Seth said bluntly. "She wrote to me two months later, to tell me she was pregnant. She sent one letter to my office, the other to this address. I never got either one. Did you by any chance intercept them?"

"Of course I did."

"Of course?" he repeated tersely.

"Some little nobody who plays the fiddle and gets herself pregnant with your child? You think I'd let her anywhere near the Talbot fortune?"

So his suspicions had been well-founded; Eleonore had cold-bloodedly destroyed two letters and thereby deprived him of any knowledge that he was about to become a father. He said at random, because he could scarcely take in her perfidy, "Lia's far from a nobody—she has an international reputation as a violinist."

"Then why didn't you know her name?" Eleonore flashed.

"She wanted to be anonymous—her fame was new to her then. I did my best to trace her, without success...if one thing's clear in all this mess, it's that Lia wasn't then, and isn't now, after my money."

"You're far too naïve! I opened the letter that came here, and went straight to your office to destroy the second one; fortunately, she'd mentioned she'd sent two."

"The child she was carrying—that was my child," Seth said harshly.

"I'm quite sure she had an abortion once she knew she wasn't getting a penny out of us."

"She didn't. My daughter—your granddaughter—is now seven years old. Her name is Marise."

"So when are you getting married, Seth, and making the child legitimate?"

Eleonore had always had the ability to get under his skin. "I'm not," Seth said, his voice rising. "You and father put me off marriage permanently. But I've been cheated out of seven years of my daughter's life because you destroyed those letters. How could you have done that?"

"Easily," Eleonore shrugged, "and I'd do it again."

"You would, wouldn't you? Luckily Lia didn't choose to emulate you and have an abortion."

Eleonore's voice was like a whiplash. "Just what do you mean by that?"

"That fight you and Father had when I was eight—I overheard it. I heard you tell him how you'd aborted his second child. A girl, you said. She would have been my sister."

"You were in bed asleep."

"I was hiding in the library, where I'd gone looking for a book. You destroyed a life because it would have inconvenienced you."

"I'd already produced an heir to the Talbot name—it was my duty to do so. But there was no need for a second child."

"Why do you think I've never married? Never wanted a child of my own? Could it possibly have anything to do with overhearing my own mother discuss how she'd cold-bloodedly rid herself of a child she considered nothing but a nuisance?"

"Don't blame me for your shortcomings!"

"Who else is there to blame?"

"Eavesdroppers get what they deserve."

"Isn't that the truth," Seth retorted, and took a deep breath. A shouting match hadn't been in his plans. He said evenly, "I want a signed confession from you, saying that you destroyed those two letters."

"Why should I do that?"

"Because if you don't, I'll make sure the information goes public."

Eleonore's breath hissed between her teeth. "You wouldn't."

"Try me."

"What will you do with it should I sign such a ridiculous document?"

"Show it to Lia. So she knows why I left her totally alone to deal with her pregnancy and our daughter."

"She's blackmailing you!"

"That's the last thing she'd ever do—Lia has ethics. Unlike you. Sign it, Mother, or I'll make sure every one of your high-class acquaintances finds out exactly what you did eight years ago. Tampering with the mail is a federal offence, by the way."

"Go to the desk and bring me my leather folder."

Seth did so, then sat like a stone as Eleonore wrote a single brief sentence on her elegant letterhead. She signed the crisp vellum, and passed it to him. "I hope that satisfies you," she said bitterly.

He read it, folded it and tucked it in his jacket pocket. "You're not even remotely sorry for what you did, are you?"

"I've already told you I'm not. Now that you've gotten what you came for, I'd suggest you leave."

"Did you ever love me?" Seth said very quietly.

Her eyes a glacial blue, she snapped, "I did my duty by you, Seth. What more do you want?"

What, indeed? Seth got to his feet, picking up his jacket and tie. "I'll let myself out," he said.

He strode out of the sitting room, closing the door with exaggerated gentleness behind him. But as he crossed the hallway, his father came out of the adjoining room. Allan Talbot was the last person Seth wanted to see right now. "Father," he said, dredging up his good manners with conventional politeness, "how are you?"

Allan had Seth's green eyes, coupled with auburn hair thickly threaded with gray; although he was nearly Seth's height, his shoulders had a perpetual stoop and his face was prematurely wrinkled. If Eleonore had seized control in their marriage, Allan had abdicated it in a way Seth had found difficult to respect; and all too often in Seth's youth, Allan had found solace in the most expensive of wines. Now Allan said with unusual forcefulness, "I need to talk to you."

"I'm in a—"

"Please, Seth."

Stifling a sigh, Seth followed Allan further down the wide hallway to the library where Allan spent most of his time. Allan closed the door behind him, shutting them in with the long-remembered odors of leather upholstery, old books and beeswax polish. "I overheard what you just told your mother," he said unevenly. "I'd seen your car outside, so I was looking for you. I never realized you knew what happened all those years ago—about the abortion, I mean. That was a terrible burden for a small boy to carry."

"It's a long time ago, Father."

"If I'd only known you'd heard every word your mother and I said…right here in this room." An old pain scored Allan's face. "That was the worst night of my life—and to find out that you witnessed it is almost more than I can bear."

"I survived," Seth said dryly. "As you see."

"I'd always wanted another child, Eleonore knew that. Once she'd told me what she'd done, I couldn't bring myself to get close to her again. To reach out to her in any way." He dashed a hand to his eyes, adding with scathing self-criticism, "I reached for the bottle instead."

"You're scarcely to be blamed."

"I wish I could agree. I couldn't bring myself to divorce her, either—what kind of man does that make me?"

"How about loyal?" Seth ventured, feeling his heart ache with unaccustomed sympathy. Had he ever really allowed himself to see his father's pain before?

"Gutless is a better word."

"You're being too harsh. The past is done with, over. Beating up on yourself doesn't accomplish anything."

"I'm not sure the past is ever over."

He, Seth, had certainly been living his life as though the past rode him like a millstone. He said awkwardly, "Why don't we change gears here, Father? You have a granddaughter now. A little girl called Marise who's seven years old and who inherited the Talbot green eyes."

Allan's eyes filmed with tears. "Have you seen her?"

"Not yet. Lia's being very protective of her, understandably so. For eight years she thought I'd abandoned any responsibility for that night in Paris and its outcome…until we met again by sheer chance a few days ago at White Cay, and it all came out in the open. But sooner or later I'm going to see Marise. I have to."

"I'd love to meet her," Allan said wistfully.

Seth took one more step into new territory. "Perhaps that can be arranged. Given time."

Clumsily Allan put an arm around his son's shoulders. "Marise," he whispered. "Such a pretty name."

"Her mother is the most beautiful woman in the world," Seth said hoarsely.

"You're in love with her."

"No, I'm not—I don't seem to have that ability. But I admire and respect her. And," Seth's smile was wry, "lust after her. That hasn't changed over the last eight years."

"Respect and passion aren't a bad basis for marriage."

"Lia doesn't want to get married."

"Then you'll have to change her mind, won't you? That shouldn't be any problem for the man who runs Talbot Holdings. Iron fist in the velvet glove, and all that."

"Lia's fists aren't what you'd call velvet and she doesn't bother with gloves," Seth said with a grin.

"She must be quite a woman."

"That's one way of describing her."

"I look forward to meeting her," Allan said. "Will you send me a photo of Marise, Seth? Of Lia, too, if you have one."

He didn't. "I'll send them to your private postbox," Seth said tautly. "Otherwise Mother'll tear them to shreds."

"What she did was unconscionable—you have every right to be angry."

"So do you."

Allan sighed. "The hard truth is, I still love her. Don't ask me why. But I do. Who knows, perhaps little Marise will cause some sort of miracle."

"I won't bring Marise into this house!"

Allan rubbed his forehead. "I'm so sorry, for so much," he said. "But you mustn't let my failings and Eleonore's keep you from your own happiness, Seth. That only compounds the tragedy."

Seth felt his throat tighten. He said roughly, "You know what? This is the nearest we've ever come to a real conversation."

Allan suddenly smiled, a smile that made him look years younger. "Good," he said. "Keep in touch, son. I'll travel anywhere at any time to meet my granddaughter."

The two men exchanged another unaccustomed hug, then Seth ran downstairs and let himself out. It was already growing dark and he had a long drive ahead of him. But plenty to think about on that drive, he realized, checking that he had the single piece of paper his mother had signed.

He was going to make sure Lia saw that piece of paper. Nor was he going to wait ten days for it to happen.

Quickly Seth punched in the numbers. The connection was made and the phone began to ring. The receiver was picked up and a woman's voice said crisply, "Lia d'Angeli."

His mouth dry, Seth said easily, "I'll meet you in half an hour at the Klimt Coffee House. It's right across from your hotel."

There was an instant of dead silence. "Seth, is this your idea of a joke?"

"We won't jump each other at the Klimt. I promise."

Lia scowled at the opposite wall of her hotel room and said the obvious. "You're in Vienna."

"Yep. Did you really think I'd wait until you came back?"

"Actually I did. Silly me. I can't meet you, I've got a rehearsal this afternoon and a concert tonight."

He kept his voice light with a huge effort. "So are you shacked up with Rosnikov?"

She made a very rude noise down the receiver. "Are you traveling with a malleable woman who never raises her voice?"

"I've discovered they bore me," he said meekly.

"And I don't?"

"Not so far."

"You have such a winning way with words."

"Spend half an hour with me and I'll see if I can improve," he said. "You can leave in lots of time for your rehearsal."

"I—dammit," she exploded, and slammed down the phone. The portrait on the opposite wall was of a plumply naked Renaissance woman with artless blue eyes and loopy blond curls; Lia glared at her and yanked open the doors of the immense baroque wardrobe in which her few clothes hung like orphans. Seth was here. In Vienna.

She didn't have to meet him.

If she didn't turn up, she wouldn't put it past him to storm the hotel.

She couldn't allow him to come to her room. It had a bed in it.

She snagged her jersey pants and tunic from the hanger; they were a rich shade of aubergine. Quickly she dressed, making up her face with care and leaving her hair loose. Then she flung a glittering silver-embroidered scarf over her shoulders and jammed silver hoops into her earlobes. The supple leather boots she'd bought in Paris were the final touch.

She looked very classy. No way was she going to let Seth Talbot know she was a mass of pre-concert nerves.

He'd be a useful distraction, she thought. Anything to make the hours pass until tonight.

Pulling a rude face at the portrait, Lia left the room. Her hotel was in the Belvedere district, near the monumental Musikverein, where she would be performing tonight. Trying to breathe slowly and deeply, as her coach had taught her, Lia walked to Karlsplatz, mentally saluting the two carved angels at the entrance to the magnificent Karlskirche. Then she stopped to smooth the curves of the Henry Moore sculptures by the pond.

The spring sunshine was warm on her face; the ducks were in an amatory mood. Why had she thought about Seth entirely too much in the past few days?

Maybe when she saw him again, she'd find some answers.

The Klimt Coffee House was one of her favorites, not the least for its fine quality reproductions of the artist's fiercely beautiful portraits of women. She could add to that the high ceilings and elegantly arched windows, the civilized murmur of conversation and the delicious odor of Turkish coffee. Her eyes flicked around the room.

Seth was seated beneath a huge reproduction of *The Kiss,* that unabashedly erotic blend of golds and reds depicting a man and a woman so entwined as to be almost indistinguishable. Her heels clicking on the marble floor, she walked toward Seth. He got up to meet her, kissing her on both cheeks.

"What's up?" he said abruptly. "You'll do fine tonight."

Scowling at him, she replied, "Is it so pitifully obvious that I'm a mass of nerves?"

"To me it is—although I've never been known for empathy."

She raised her brows. "Well," she remarked, "I should've realized we wouldn't waste time with small talk…I'll have a Turkish coffee and a big slice of Sachertorte."

"Chocolate cake layered with apricot jam?" Seth said, amused. "You're in a bad way."

She was rhythmically tapping the tabletop with her fingernails; he'd never found her to be a jittery woman. "It's always this way before a concert," she said. "I'll be fine once I start to play."

"So there's a cost to being the best."

"Right now I'm not convinced it's worth it."

Seth dropped his hand over hers, stilling her restless movements. "I wish I could help."

Very briefly her fingers curled into his palm. A wicked glint in her eye, she said, "You're distracting me. That helps."

He raised her hand to his lips, kissing her fingers one by one. "A man's gotta do what a man's gotta do."

Her cheeks, which had been too pale, were now patched with hectic color. Flustered, she said, "You gotta order my cake, that's what you gotta do."

"Lia, you disappoint me—you'd choose Sachertorte over seduction?" Seth said, grinning as he signaled the waiter. After he'd given their order, he drew a plain white envelope from his jacket pocket, his smile fading. "This is for you."

She took the envelope from him as warily as if it were a

poisonous snake. Then, with sudden decisiveness, she tore it open and read the words on the single sheet of embossed notepaper. "Your mother destroyed both of my letters," she said blankly.

"Yes. I wish to God she hadn't."

Lia's own mother, for all her enormous professionalism and high standards, had always loved her only child and wished the best for her. "How could your mother have done that? Intervened so cruelly—altered the course of three lives, one of them her own son's?"

"I don't know, Lia—I don't have the answer."

"It was a vicious thing to do," Lia said faintly. "All those weeks I waited for you to get in touch with me, and tried so hard not to hate you...then feeling utterly alone when Marise was born..."

Her eyes were shining with tears. "I'd have been there for you, had I known," Seth said hoarsely. "I swear it, Lia."

"But you didn't know, because your mother destroyed my letters. Why, Seth? Why?"

He'd realized this question would arise; realized, too, that to attempt an answer would be to reveal things about himself he'd always kept private. Stumbling a little at first, Seth began to describe the stone mansion, Eleonore's coldness, Allan's subservience and his own escape as a boy to the woods and the shore. The waiter brought their order, and still he talked, encouraged by Lia's complete and unforced attention. Then he looked up, knowing he was making a momentous decision. "Do you remember I asked you, when I found out about Marise, if you'd considered having an abortion?"

"Yes. You looked...overwhelmed when I told you I hadn't."

He forced himself to keep going. "When I was eight my mother had one...I think it broke my father's heart when he found out. I overheard them the night she told him."

This time Lia covered his hand with hers. "Seth, I'm so sorry," she whispered.

"I can't ever thank you enough for having Marise," he said in a raw voice, "just as I'll always regret I wasn't there for you."

A tear dropped from her dark lashes to the back of his hand. He gazed at it, seeing how the light from the chandelier had refracted into a tiny rainbow in its midst. Why had he told her something he'd kept secret for years? And why did a single tear feel like the most precious of gifts? "This is the last thing we should be talking about when you've got a concert tonight," he muttered.

"Is it? Why, Seth?"

"Because I've upset you."

"You trusted me enough to share what must have been a huge trauma for a little boy," she said in a low voice.

"Telling you hasn't changed anything."

"Change happens, whether you want it to or not," she said implacably. "Do you have a ticket for the concert?"

"No. I prefer CDs. Music at a distance."

"I'll see there's a ticket at the door for you."

His eyes narrowed; if she could throw down a gauntlet, so could he. "When do I get to meet Marise?"

"I haven't told her about you yet."

A knife seemed to have lodged in his gut. "You haven't? Why not?"

She said defensively, "I wanted to hear about the letters first."

"Is that the only reason?"

Her lashes dropped to hide her eyes. "When I got back from the Caribbean, it was all too new—I had to deal with my own feelings first."

He purposely didn't ask what those feelings were. "But you won't keep me from her?"

"I don't know." Fury smoldered in her eyes. "Am I supposed to ignore what your mother did?"

"I'm not responsible for my mother's actions," Seth said tightly.

"She's part of your family. Her, and your father."

"He wants to meet Marise, too."

Lia was rapping her nails on the table again. Was she in danger of blaming Seth for his mother's crimes? "I can't deal with this right now."

"I shouldn't have shown you my mother's confession. The timing's lousy."

"I'm the one who demanded proof. I can scarcely complain when I get it."

"You can complain all you like," Seth said. "For seven years you were a single mother as a direct result of my mother's actions. How the hell do you think that makes me feel?"

"I have no idea," Lia said tautly. "You're far too adept at keeping your feelings hidden."

With no idea where the words came from, Seth said, "I'll go to the concert."

Letting out her breath in a tiny sigh, Lia angled the last mouthful of luscious chocolate icing onto her fork. She'd learned a great deal about Seth in the last few minutes: information that only served to bind him closer to her, in ways that both intrigued and terrified her. Frowning, she said, "Why do men have to be so complicated?"

"To keep women guessing. Want another piece of cake?"

"I wouldn't get into my dress if I did. It's a very slinky dress, and you can come to the reception after the concert if you want to."

"Providing we leave it together."

She raised her brows. "Autocratic, aren't you?"

"When it suits me."

"So you want a commitment from me."

"Only about the reception."

"You've made it all too clear you won't commit yourself

to me in any other way. But if I let you anywhere near Marise, you can't operate like that with her."

"I won't," he said harshly. "That's a promise."

Could she believe him? Was she in Karlsplatz, Vienna, sitting across the table from the man who'd been haunting her dreams? "Suppose I allow you to see Marise," she said. "Suppose you and she develop a relationship, and in the course of that, you and I end up having an affair. What happens when you get tired of me, Seth?"

"We'll deal with it when it happens."

"I won't be dumped like so much garbage."

"I won't dump you like you're garbage!"

"Well, that got a reaction," Lia said.

He ran his fingers around his collar. "I'd like to be in bed with you right now."

"One of my professors at Juilliard said in class one day, peering at us over the rims of his glasses, *No sex before a concert. It drains the music of its passion.* Too bad, Seth."

"So by abstaining, I'm doing my bit for Brahms?"

"We all have to sacrifice for art."

"You can always make me laugh," Seth said in a voice of discovery. "Sex and laughter—that's quite a combo."

"Almost as good as Turkish coffee and chocolate cake." Lia pushed back her chair. "I've got to go. The rehearsal's in a couple of hours and I do breathing exercises beforehand."

"A concert brings you face to face with yourself," he ventured.

Surprised and pleased that he'd understood, she said, "That's right—what do I have to give to the music? Will it find me wanting?" Her mouth quirked. "Minor little questions like that."

Seth got to his feet, and, ignoring the other customers, kissed her full on the mouth. "You couldn't possibly disappoint yourself, the audience or the music," he said. Reaching in his pocket, he took out a small box. "This is for you," he added, not meeting her eyes. "To bring you luck tonight."

She was staring at the box, making no move to take it. "Seth, I can't take a gift from you."

"Why not? Do you think I'm trying to bribe you?"

"Of course not." She looked right at him. "You're as different from your mother as you can be."

He pushed the box toward her, more affected by her simple endorsement than he cared to show. "Open it, Lia…it's nothing much."

She took the box and flipped the lid up. Earrings, each a single, multifaceted diamond, flashed colored fire in a bed of black velvet. "They're gorgeous," she exclaimed. "But—"

"They reminded me of you." His crooked smile made her, inexplicably, want to weep. "When you feel passionately about something, even your hair seems to spark."

She blurted, "I should have believed you about the letters without having to have proof—I'm truly sorry I didn't."

"You're forgiven," he said lightly.

Lia took a deep breath. "The earrings are lovely, Seth, I'll be happy to wear them tonight…thank you."

He kissed her again. "Too many sexy paintings in this room—you'd better go. I'll stay here for a while and read the paper. *Auf Wiedersehen,* beautiful Lia."

Her cheeks were bright scarlet, clashing with her outfit. She made a sound that would have translated in any language as *humph,* and walked out of the coffeehouse with perfect aplomb.

A foolish smile plastered on his face, Seth sat down again. He'd given a woman diamonds, revealed a lifelong secret and agreed to go to a concert. None of these behaviors was typical of him.

And he was going to leave the reception with Lia.

The professor hadn't said she couldn't have sex after the concert.

CHAPTER TEN

AFTER the intermission, the orchestra tuned their instruments, then silence fell over the house. Seth sat still in his box seat, his eyes glued to the stage, which was crowded with tuxedoed musicians. He felt as nervous as if it were he who was about to play.

All this time Lia had been waiting backstage. How did she stand it?

In a tap of high heels Lia walked out onto the stage, followed by Ivor Rosnikov and the conductor. She was wearing a smoky purple satin dress with inserts in the full-length skirt that were filled with tiny pleats; they kicked out as she moved. Her bare arms were pale as ivory, her hair drawn back severely from her face. The diamond earrings he'd given her sparkled in her lobes.

The conductor adjusted the score, Rosnikov settled himself at his cello, and after a quick glance at his two soloists, the conductor raised his baton. The orchestra played the first somber, flowing notes. Seth sat very still, waiting. Lia, also waiting, looked indrawn and remote.

Why would she need him, Seth, when she had her music? She'd never fall in love with him; at least he was safe from that complication.

As the orchestra fell silent, Rosnikov began to play a rich, sonorous melody. Lia raised her bow and joined him, the two instruments separating only to blend, blending only to separate. She and Ivor, Seth saw in an uprush of heated and primitive emotion, were also completely in tune with each other, making frequent eye contact in a way that seemed to him immensely intimate.

He, Seth, could never share such intimacy with Lia; he was, in comparison with Ivor Rosnikov, a musical ignoramus.

The cellist was, subtly, both more handsome and younger-looking in the flesh than in his publicity photos. The emotion that was surging through Seth was jealousy.

He'd never in his life been jealous of another man. For a very simple reason: he'd never cared enough about a woman to feel jealous.

Lia was different. Hadn't he known that from the first moment he'd laid eyes on her?

The wonderfully lyrical second movement swept to its conclusion, followed by a joyful finale that brought a smile to Lia's face; it was achingly obvious that she was doing exactly what she'd been born to do. The final triumphant chords filled the magnificent hall; there was an instant of total and respectful silence before the audience erupted into a storm of applause.

Lia and Ivor had linked hands; the conductor stepped down from the podium, kissing Lia on the cheek. Ivor then leaned over and kissed her full on the mouth, his hands clasping her waist. Seth's fingers dug into his palms. How dare he?

Not that Lia looked as though she was objecting to this public display of—what? Affection? Mutual achievement? Or just plain sex? Rosnikov's dark locks and romantically pale face had women flocking to him the length of Europe. Why should Lia be immune?

The last thing Seth wanted to do was stand around at a stuffy reception watching Ivor Rosnikov drape himself all over Lia; and simultaneously having to subdue the urge to throttle, publicly, a world-famous cellist. Would Lia even miss him if he didn't go? He very much doubted that she would.

He, Seth, was superfluous to her world. That was what he'd learned tonight by attending her concert. But was running away from that world an option?

He'd never been one to back down from a challenge. Seth went to the reception, where he downed a glass of inferior champagne and disdained to join the crowd that eddied around Lia and Ivor, and that included members of the media whose flashlights went off with monotonous regularity. The whole time, the cellist's arm lay over Lia's bare shoulders. Throttling Rosnikov began to seem entirely too merciful. For the sake of his sanity, Seth wandered over to a group of acquaintances on the far side of the room, stood with his back to Lia and talked about the economy as though his life depended on it.

Gradually the crowd thinned. Then, behind him, Seth heard the click of heels on the marble floor. As he turned, Lia said, "Ivor, I'd like you to meet my friend, Seth Talbot…as I mentioned, Seth and I are going out together after the reception. Seth, Ivor Rosnikov."

Seth had to admire her gall. He smiled at the cellist and produced some conventional words of congratulation about the concert. "How is it you know Lia?" Ivor asked in his heavily accented English.

"We met some time ago," Seth said casually. "Though we've seen nothing of each other for years."

"Yet you take her out tonight?"

"Yes," said Seth, "I'm taking her out tonight."

"Then I am—how do you say?—the loser," Ivor said, and with elaborate gallantry raised Lia's hand to his lips. "I will see you in Hamburg the day after tomorrow, *liebchen*," he said, smiling deep into her eyes. Baring his teeth at Seth, he added, "You will look after her. Late hours are not good."

"I'm sure Lia is quite capable of deciding how late she'll stay out," Seth said amicably. Punching the guy on the nose instead of throttling him wouldn't do, either. Bad publicity for all concerned.

Ten minutes later, he and Lia were walking into the cool of a spring night outside the imposing terra-cotta and cream façade of Musikverein. She glanced around to check that they were alone. "Where are we going?"

"Do you want highbrow, lowbrow or somewhere in between?"

"Middle. With grub and a dance floor."

"Okay. Want to walk?"

"Providing it's not halfway across Vienna, yes." Falling into step beside him, yet preserving a careful distance between them, Lia added, "What did you think of the concert?"

"You played extraordinarily well," he said truthfully.

"I missed a note in the 54th bar of the third movement."

"I didn't notice," he said dryly.

"You didn't like Ivor."

"Any more than Ivor liked me."

"You looked like a couple of roosters about to square off."

She looked as belligerent as a rooster herself. "How long were you his lover?" Seth asked. "Or are you still?"

"What are you—the lawyer for the prosecution?"

"You sure weren't objecting to being kissed by him in full view of two thousand people."

It had been a very long day. "What was I supposed to do?" Lia retorted. "Whack him with my violin?"

"Is he a good lover?"

"I wouldn't know—since I've never been his lover. Apart from anything else, his ego's so big there'd be no room for me."

"You and I are in perfect agreement on that point," Seth growled, and smothered a relief strong enough for ten men.

Lia stopped on the sidewalk, her dark eyes level. "You congratulated Ivor for his playing. But I had to ask before you'd tell me what you thought about mine."

He'd hurt her; that was what she was saying. "You think I was going to bare my soul in front of that Paganini lookalike?"

"So bare it now."

"Dammit, Lia, I felt the way I always feel when you play—only more so because you were right there in front of me. The club we're going to is just down here."

She planted her feet. "Keep talking—how do you always feel?"

"As though you know me through and through. As though all my defenses are useless and my soul an open book. Is that what you want to know?" he said furiously.

She bit her lip. "Don't hate me for it."

"Why don't you give me a list of your various lovers in the last eight years—in case I meet up with any of them at one of these fancy receptions."

She drew her lacy white shawl closer around her shoulders. "No list. No lovers."

"Oh, sure."

She said irritably, "I need to sit down, take off my shoes, have at least two lagers and a big plate of *rindsgulasch* with extra dumplings. Are you or are you not taking me to this club?"

He seized her by the elbow. "You must have had a lover—it was eight years, Lia!"

"I know how long it was. I was a single mother most of that time, remember?"

"There were lots of times when you were on the opposite side of the Atlantic from your daughter. Free to bed whom you pleased."

The music she'd played was still coursing through her veins. Lia said flatly, "I discovered passion with you and I wasn't about to settle for less."

He felt as though she'd just hit him hard in the chest with a double bass. "Is that true?"

"I try not to tell lies. Lager and dumplings, Seth."

Reeling, Seth tucked her arm through his and walked the last two blocks in silence. The club was crowded and noisy. Skillfully Seth threaded through the patrons to an empty table near the dance floor, got the waiter's attention and placed their order. "Shoes off yet?" he said economically.

"You bet. Do you believe me?"

"About the lovers? Yes."

"Good."

He'd have hated hearing the names of her lovers; equally, he'd hated being told there'd been none. Because it scared the pants off him to find out she'd been faithful to him for eight long years?

He was a yellow-bellied coward, Seth thought scathingly, watching as the waiter brought two tankards of beer and set them on the table, the froth overflowing. Lia raised hers and drank deep, the muscles moving in her throat as she swallowed.

Her exquisite, ivory-smooth throat.

She said edgily, "Is something wrong?"

"Did you fall in love with me in Paris?"

"No," she said. "But it was as far from casual as it could be. And not just because of Marise."

Wasn't the same true for him? But he'd gotten his life back on track, finally, and there it had remained ever since. Until he'd seen her in her turquoise suit swimming as gracefully as a dolphin in the sea.

Seth took a big slug of beer. "Have you ever fallen in love?"

"No," Lia said, her fingers tightening around the tankard. She wasn't going to start now by falling in love with Seth, either. She'd be out of her mind to do that. The man was as barricaded as a fortress.

"You've got your music—no room for a mere man alongside that."

"That's not true," she said sharply. "I love Marise with all my heart…why should a man be any different?"

Was he now going to be jealous of a seven-year-old child? With a sigh of exasperation Seth took another gulp of beer. "Let's change the subject."

"Better still, let's dance."

Discovering he craved action, too, Seth led her out onto the crowded floor, where to the raunchy blast of disco and the flash of strobes, they gyrated and swung. Her hair began to slip from its pins; her body, in the clinging satin of her gown, was unbearably sexy. He was going to end the evening in her bed, thought Seth. But this time, it would be a controlled decision with no postmortems.

He leaned closer to Lia, raising his voice. "Our food's arrived."

She gave him a brilliant smile, twirled and fell back into his arms. "Lead me to it."

Yeah, he thought. In bed, that's where we belong.

At their table, Lia tucked into her stew and dumplings, washing it down with liberal quantities of lager. "Luscious," she said, licking her fork. "I want dessert now. *Apfelstrudel.* Warm with whipped cream on top and a big glass of Riesling to go with it."

"A woman of immoderate appetites."

She leaned over and kissed him with sensuous pleasure. "Dumplings, lager and you."

"In that order?"

"Tonight."

"Is this how you always relax after a concert?"

She laughed. "I usually go back to my hotel room and pace the floor, agonizing over all the mistakes I made. This is much more fun."

Pink Floyd throbbed through the smoky air. "It ain't exactly Brahms."

"We could dance again."

Seth ordered dessert and a bottle of Riesling, and this time took Lia in his arms on the dance floor. They were the only couple in formal clothes in the entire club and he, too, was having fun.

Not a word his parents had understood.

The level of Riesling sank in the bottle, Lia drinking most of it. The wine loosened her tongue. She talked about the ups and downs of her career and the costs to her personal life; she described some of the hilarious contretemps of working with autocratic conductors and temperamental pianists; noticeably, she didn't talk about Marise. She also flagged the waiter and ordered a double crème de menthe, a choice that made Seth shudder. He, by now, was drinking coffee. One of them ought to stay sober, he thought, amused that she simply became wittier as her words began, very slightly, to slur. "Lia," he said finally, "I think I should take you back to your hotel. Ivor wouldn't approve of the lateness of the hour."

"I'm flying to Hamburg at noon."

"You and your hangover."

She blinked at him. "Am I drunk?"

"A reasonable facsimile thereof."

"Don't use such big words," she said querulously.

"Okay. You're pretty close to plastered."

"It's all your fault."

"Yeah?"

"I have no idea what to do about you."

"Welcome to the club," Seth said wryly.

She gave him a big smile. "You're really cute, though."

Lia, sober, would never use a word like cute. "Thank you," Seth said solemnly.

"But I sure don't like your family." She swallowed the last of the sticky green liqueur, licking the rim of the glass. "Every now and then it hits me, what your mother did. The pain she caused because she was afraid I'd sink my sharp little claws into her money…aren't you absolutely furious with her?"

"Yes," said Seth, not liking the way the conversation had turned.

"Yes," Lia mimicked. "Is that all you can say?"

"You think I'm totally unfeeling?" Seth said violently. "I can hardly bear to think about it. About you, alone with a new baby, thinking I didn't even care enough to pick up the phone—for God's sake, Lia, give me a break."

Lia looked at him owlishly. "I pushed a button there."

Seth scowled at her. "You're cut off. Black coffee from now on."

"Ugh—at this time of night?"

"In that case, it's time to leave."

She wrinkled her nose. "I'm in the mood to seduce you. 'Cause the only time I'm not confused is when we're in bed together."

"That goes for me, too."

"I love what we do in bed," she said chirpily.

Their neighbors at the next table were unabashedly listening. "So do I," said Seth.

"Why are we sitting here, then?"

Seth dealt with the bill and got up, tucking her shawl around her shoulders. She lurched to her feet. "Ouch," she said, "I wish they'd turn off the strobes, they're making me dizzy."

Seth, wisely, didn't suggest that lager, Riesling and crème de menthe might have some connection to dizziness. He put an arm firmly around Lia's waist, steered her toward the door and quickly flagged a taxi; she was in no shape to walk. In the back seat, she put her head on his shoulder and fell instantly asleep.

None of the malleable women he'd dated had ever drunk too much. Neither had they played their guts out in front of two thousand people; or made love with Lia's generosity and wild abandon.

By the time he got Lia to her hotel room, she was paper-pale. "I sh—shouldn't have had the crème de menthe," she muttered and headed for the bathroom. Seth turned down the bed, found her deliciously lacy nightgown under the pillow and briefly held it to his face. He wanted to see her wearing it; then strip it from her body. But tonight wasn't the night.

When she next made love with him, she was going to be wide-awake and fully aware of what she was doing.

He wrote her a quick note, propping it up on the bedside table. Then she emerged from the bathroom, sagged into his arms and said muzzily, "Your eyes are the same color as crème de menthe. Turn off the light and come to bed with me."

Seth made a soothing and noncommittal noise in his throat as he pulled her evening dress over her head. Her silk underwear made his head swim; swiftly he unclasped her bra and slipped the nightgown on. As he eased her down on the bed, he noticed with huge tenderness that her dark lashes were already drifting to her cheeks. After peeling off her stockings, he covered her with the blanket. "Sleep well, darling Lia," he said.

But Lia was already asleep.

At nine o'clock the next morning, a knock came at Lia's door. She peered through the peephole, already knowing who it would be. "Good morning, Seth," she said pleasantly.

His jaw tight, he thrust a newspaper at her. "Have you seen this?"

"Yes. Don't worry about it. It happened once before and the fuss died down in no time."

On the front page of the tabloid, beneath a color photo of Rosnikov kissing Lia, were inch-tall headlines insinuating that the cellist was the father of Lia's child. "Don't worry about it?" Seth snarled. "My daughter's being subjected to the gutter press and all you can say is don't worry about it?"

"This is Austria. Not New York. No one at home will see

it," Lia said reasonably, wishing her headache would go away. Not that she didn't deserve the headache. She was never going near crème de menthe again.

Trying to change the subject, she added, "The reviews of the concert were good, weren't they?"

"Lia, I won't tolerate this kind of gossip about Marise."

"Why are you so upset? It's my problem, not yours."

He felt as though she'd punched him, hard. "Marise is my daughter, too—don't you think it's about time you admitted that? I'm going to meet her, Lia. Whether you want me to or not." Allan, his father, might have allowed Eleonore to walk all over him. He, Seth, wasn't about to let Lia do the same. Marise was too important. Too essential, he thought, and wondered where that particular word had come from.

"We'll see," Lia said, her jaw a stubborn jut.

"Don't try and stop me," he said very quietly. "You'll regret it if you do."

"Are you threatening me?"

"I'm telling you the truth."

"You're forgetting that Marise has a say here," Lia pointed out. Poking the tabloid with one finger, she added, "In the meantime, you're blowing this way out of proportion."

"It's untenable—a seven-year-old's name smeared on the front page of a cheap rag."

Her nostrils flared. Her temper rose to meet his. "So what am I supposed to do? Marry Rosnikov just to keep the newspapers quiet?"

"Marry me, instead," Seth said.

The words echoed in his head. What in hell had possessed him to say them? He didn't want to marry Lia. He didn't want to marry anyone.

"No, thanks," she said.

Did she have to answer so promptly? Did he mean so little to her that a proposal of marriage didn't even make her blink? "So much for that idea," he said sarcastically.

"Oh, come off it," she flared. "If I'd said yes, you'd be clocking a four-minute mile to the airport right now."

That she was probably right only infuriated him all the more. "That's precisely where I'm going…I'll call you on the fifteenth and we'll set up a meeting with Marise. Who, I sincerely hope, will remain ignorant of all this garbage." He tossed the tabloid onto Lia's bed.

"I protect her from as much of the world's garbage as I can," Lia snapped. "But I'm not omnipotent, Seth. The world exists, and all children have to lose their innocence." Her face suddenly changed. "As you did," she whispered, resting one hand on his sleeve. "I'm so sorry, I wasn't thinking."

The last thing Seth wanted was sympathy. He picked up her hand and let it drop by her side. "I hope Hamburg goes well," he said coldly.

"I'll say hello to Ivor for you."

Her cheeks were bright pink with temper. Seth planted a very angry kiss full on her lips, feeling heat rip through his body straight to his loins. Then he turned on his heel and left the room, shutting the door with a definitive snap.

He ran down the stairs at a reckless speed and strode through the lobby into the spring sunshine. He'd had more than enough of Vienna. Manhattan, he thought. That's where he was going next. Home, where he knew which way was up.

CHAPTER ELEVEN

"LET'S go see the daffodils, Mum."

"Sure," Lia said, smiling fondly at her daughter. Marise was wearing her new yellow boots and slicker, her brown curls tucked under a sou'wester. Lia took her own slicker off the hook and grabbed an umbrella before they walked outdoors.

She took a deep breath. Wet soil, new leaves and the promise of spring. If only she could simply enjoy it.

But she couldn't. She had to tell Marise about Seth.

He wasn't going to go away. Not this time.

Trying to calm her nerves, Lia waited until she and Marise were kneeling down picking some of the daffodils that bloomed among the birch trees. Rain pattered on the umbrella. "Marise," she said, "I have some big news for you."

"Did I pass my math test?"

Lia laughed ruefully. "You aced English, that's all I know. This is about something else."

Marise had always been sensitive to shades of feeling. She buried her nose in a wet yellow trumpet, her green eyes wary. "You're not sick like Mary Blunden's mother, are you?"

"No, I'm fine—I was talking to Mrs. Blunden yesterday and she's getting out of hospital very soon, so that's good news. This is about something else. It's about your father, Marise."

Marise's dark lashes, so like her mother's, dropped to hide her eyes. "What about him?"

"Years ago, when I realized I was pregnant with you, I wrote and told him about you. He never answered my letters."

"He didn't want me," Marise said with irrefutable logic.

"That's what I thought at the time. But I was wrong. Someone took the letters before he could read them. So it wasn't his fault that he never got in touch with me."

"How'd you find that out?" Marise asked with a touch of belligerence.

"I met him again, by chance, when I was at White Cay. Then I saw him last week in Vienna. He showed me proof about the letters. I couldn't let you go on thinking he stayed away from you on purpose because he didn't care about you—that's not true."

"Oh," said Marise. Methodically she started shredding the petals from a daffodil. "Will he come to my school? So the other kids can see I've got a real dad?"

Lia's heart clenched. Feeling her way, she said, "Would you like him to do that?"

"Mmm...I'm the only one in the whole school who doesn't have a father somewhere. The kids tease me sometimes, and call me names."

Lia could imagine all too easily what those names might be. "You've never told me that before," she said with careful restraint.

"What was the use?"

What indeed? Lia snapped off a white narcissus and added it to her bouquet. It would seem the decision had been made for her: she had to allow Seth to meet Marise, for her daughter's sake. "I expect he'd go to your school," she said. "He really wants to meet you."

Marise sat down hard on the wet ground. "I won't know what to say to him."

"He may not know what to say to you, either. Not the first time. But, providing you're willing, he'd like to keep on seeing you—he's based in Manhattan, so you could get together quite often if you wanted to."

"All three of us."

"Sometimes I wouldn't be there," Lia said casually.

"Are you going to marry him?"

"No." With a nasty clench of her stomach, Lia remembered how Seth had asked her to marry him, and how quickly she'd brushed him off.

"What's his name?"

"Seth Talbot."

Marise now looked frightened. "He'll change everything."

Lia could have denied this. But within appropriate bounds, she'd always tried to tell her daughter the truth. "He'll change some things, yes."

"Does he look like me?"

Lia had been prepared for this, and had gone on the Internet for a photo of Seth. She'd zoomed in on him, and printed his image in full color. He was standing in his office in a pinstriped suit, the Manhattan skyline in the background. His thick blond hair looking encouragingly untidy; his eyes were a startlingly clear green. "That's him," Lia said.

"He's awfully big."

"He's tall, yes. But he's not mean, not like Tommy Evans. He'd be good to you, sugarplum."

Tommy Evans was the local bully. "His eyes are like mine. If he's so great, why don't you want to marry him?"

"You have to be in love to get married."

Marise frowned at the photo. "Am I s'posed to love him?"

Her daughter had a penchant for asking difficult questions. "Love isn't instant—it takes time. Perhaps you could start out by liking him. We could meet him in Stoneybrook, at the café there—you always enjoy their tuna melt sandwich."

Marise looked even more frightened. "When?"

"I'll call him when we go back to the house. How about Saturday for lunch?"

"I—I guess so. Can I tell Suzy about him? And show her the photo?"

Suzy was Marise's best friend. "Sure you can," Lia said and passed over the photo, watching as Marise jammed it into the pocket of her slicker.

"Can I go see Suzy now?"

"Just for a little while. Then you have homework to do."

Motherhood, so Lia had already discovered, meant accepting that her daughter might possibly tell Suzy more about her feelings than she'd tell Lia. They walked through the woods to the adjoining property, where Suzy lived, talking about anything other than Seth, Marise clutching a bouquet of daffodils for Suzy's mother. Then Lia went back home. Not giving herself time to think, she picked up the phone and dialed Seth's private line at work.

"Talbot," he barked.

"This is Lia."

Seth's heart did an Olympic high jump in his chest. "It's only the fourteenth."

"I talked to Marise today. We'll meet you for lunch at the Maplewood Café in Stoneybrook. On Saturday. Would noon give you enough time to get there?"

A lump the size of a small mountain had lodged itself in his throat. "Yes," he said, "I'll be there."

Quickly she gave him directions. He said choppily, "Does she want to meet me?"

"She's scared. Wary. But she'll be fine."

"Not half as scared as I am," Seth said.

"You'll both be fine."

"Last time I talked to you, you were hellbent on keeping me a thousand miles away from her—what happened?"

"She wants you to go to her school. So the kids know she's got a real dad just like everyone else." Lia's voice faltered. "They've been calling her names, Seth—I didn't know anything about it until today."

Seth's expletive hung in the air. "Children can be crueler than any adult ever thought of being."

"Will you do that for her?"

"Sure I will." It wasn't the best time for Seth to realize he'd do anything for Lia's daughter. He said abruptly, "How was Hamburg?"

"Once I got over the hangover, it went well."

"Whenever you look into my eyes are you going to be reminded of crème de menthe?"

"Time will tell."

His voice hardened. "I notice you're not suggesting we meet at Meadowland."

It would have made more sense, giving them all some much-needed privacy. "No…I'm not ready for you to be here yet."

"Have I got to earn the right?"

She flinched at the bite in his voice. "I don't know. I just don't know."

Quite suddenly he'd had enough. "Saturday at noon," he said brusquely. "I'll get there a bit early so I don't keep Marise waiting."

Lia said stiffly, "That's a good idea. Goodbye, Seth."

"Bye."

She plunked the receiver back in its cradle and stared at the raindrops weeping down the windowpane. Three days from now she'd see Seth again. But she wouldn't be able to touch him, or speak to him privately.

She'd be sharing him with Marise.

Marise's fingers were cold in Lia's as they walked into the café with its cheerful decor of ruffled curtains and checkered tablecloths. Seth was sitting at the table by the window that offered the most privacy. He got to his feet as he saw them come in the door.

Lia threaded her way across the room, smiling at a couple of acquaintances. He said easily, "Lia…nice to see you," leaned over and kissed her on the cheek. Then he hunkered down and smiled at Marise. "Hello, Marise," he said softly. "We should have met a long time before this…I'm sorry we didn't."

Marise gazed at him with her big green eyes; they were, Lia saw, giving nothing away. "Mum told me about the letters. Why did somebody do that?"

It didn't occur to him to lie. "My mother had very definite ideas about the woman I should marry, and your mother wasn't it. So she destroyed your mother's letters to me."

"Just like in a book," Marise said. "She was the villain."

"I guess so."

"The kids at school tease me 'cause I don't have a father."

Seth grimaced. "I'm sorry about that, too. Very sorry."

Marise glanced up at her mother. "Can I have a tuna melt sandwich and a chocolate milkshake?"

"Sure," Lia said. "But we'd better give Seth the chance to read the menu."

He'd practically memorized it while he was waiting for them. "I'm going to have a chicken burger with fries and coffee."

"Fries are bad for you," Marise said primly.

"Marise…" Lia said.

"They are. Miss Brenton said so in health class."

"Miss Brenton is right," Seth said. "But sometimes I break the rules. Do you ever break the rules, Marise?"

She wriggled in her seat and said with killing politeness, "That's a secret between me and my friend Suzy. Do you have a best friend?"

"A good friend of mine lives in Berlin. He introduced me to classical music a couple of years ago."

"So you don't see him very often," Marise said crushingly.

"Not as often as I'd like."

"Suzy lives next door."

That seemed to be the end of that particular conversation. To his huge relief Seth saw the waitress approach. They all gave their orders, then into the silence Lia said, "Seth loves to swim, Marise."

"I can do the backstroke," Marise said.

"Where do you swim?" Seth asked.

"We have a pool at home."

Lia smiled. "I won the Finlandia competition last year. Sibelius paid for our pool."

"When you do the backstroke," Seth said, "it's hard to see where you're going."

"Not if you look over your shoulder."

Lia said easily, "Here comes your milkshake, Marise. You're getting pretty good at diving, too."

"I don't have to hold my nose anymore."

The conversation labored on, relieved by the arrival of the food. It was horribly clear to Seth that Marise wasn't giving him an inch...and why should she? For years his absence had caused her grief. Intertwined with grief, he'd be willing to bet, was anger. He was turning into a child psychologist, he thought mockingly, as he tucked into his fries.

Marise was eyeing them. He said mildly, "Help yourself if you want a couple, Marise. Lia, did you tell me you're doing some recording soon?"

"The week after next. Until then, I have eight whole days off...pure luxury."

"You work too hard," he said roughly.

"You never do," she said, raising her brows.

She was casually dressed in jeans and a ribbed sweater that

clung to her breasts; he did his best to keep his eyes on her face. "I've been known to. Do you have to work hard at school, Marise?"

As a kid, hadn't he always hated grown-ups who asked dumb questions about school?

"Sometimes."

Lia began describing some of her daughter's English compositions, doing her best to oil the wheels. Seth, she could see, was trying as hard as he could to reach Marise in some way; it wasn't his fault he wasn't succeeding.

She was finally beginning to understand how deeply the lack of a father had marked Marise. What a mess this all is, she thought wretchedly, and started describing the competition Marise had won for a poem she'd written about raccoons. Marise said nothing.

Dessert was ordered, arrived and was eaten. Lia said brightly, "Well, I guess we should get going. Suzy's coming for a sleepover tonight."

Seth had hoped lunch might end with him and his daughter taking a little walk down the pretty main street of Stoneybrook; but now he knew better than to suggest it. He said, "Perhaps next time you could come to Manhattan with your mum, Marise? Have you ever gone to the Children's Museum?"

Marise nodded, staring down at her plate. "It's a neat place," she said in a small voice.

"Let's work on that, then," Seth said. He leaned forward, gently lifting her chin. "I know this is difficult for you—it's difficult for all of us, but especially for you. I'll do the very best I can to be a good father to you. But it'll take time for us to get used to each other. To trust each other."

"Will you come to school sometime? So the kids can see you're real?"

He fought back the sting of tears. "Of course. Anytime you want and as often as you want."

"Okay."

The child looked as though she, too, was on the verge of tears. Seth pushed back his chair, paid for lunch and led the way out of the café. On the sidewalk he said calmly, "Lia, I'll talk to you soon. Bye for now, Marise."

Then he watched as Lia drove away. Marise didn't wave.

He was exhausted, he realized, getting behind the wheel of his beloved red Porsche. It was easier to merge two corporations than to make contact with a seven-year-old who didn't want to make contact.

Would he ever reach her?

Lia, he was almost sure, hadn't been pleased when he'd suggested she bring Marise to Manhattan; certainly he'd given her no chance to argue.

Too bad, he thought heartlessly. If he wanted to make contact with Marise, didn't he also want more from Lia?

If only he knew what.

He was going back to his brownstone and spending the evening listening to Lia's CDs. If that was a maudlin and generally useless thing to do, so what?

The dazzling pyrotechnics of a Paganini violin concerto were rollicking through his living room when the phone rang. He picked it up. "Seth Talbot."

"Good taste in music," Lia said.

"The best." Discovering he was grinning like a mad fool, he added, "What's up?"

There was a short silence. "I didn't want you blaming yourself for what happened today," she said stiffly.

"What didn't happen, you mean. I'll admit to feeling god-awful as I drove home. It'll take time, Lia. That's all."

The silence was longer this time. Then Lia said in a rush, "Would you like to spend next weekend at Meadowland?"

Once again, she'd taken him completely by surprise. Wishing he could see her face, he croaked, "You mean that?"

"Yes."

"What made you change your mind?"

"I can't keep you and Marise apart—it would be wrong of me to even try. I never realized how desperate she was for a father figure…I feel so guilty, Seth."

"I'm the one who should feel guilty."

"No, you're not. Your mother should."

"Good luck," he said.

In a low voice Lia went on, "I watched you today with Marise. You were trying so hard to reach her, yet you never overstepped her boundaries. You'll make a very good father."

For the second time in one day, Seth felt the prick of tears. "Thanks," he said gruffly. "I wish Marise agreed with you."

"Maybe if you come here, it'll help."

"Marise and a big wad of guilt—are they the only reasons you're inviting me?"

"I—I don't know."

"Come clean, Lia."

Sounding thoroughly exasperated, she said, "Every time I see you, I see more layers. More depths. When I was partway plastered, I said you confused me. You still do. But you also intrigue me—I want to know what makes you tick. I shouldn't even be telling you this, my tongue has a nasty habit of running away with me…but I really like you, Seth."

Something moved in his chest, physically, as though a weight had been lifted. "I like you, too," he said huskily.

"Since we're Marise's parents, it's just as well, don't you think?" she said, a new lightness in her tone.

"So are we going to stop fighting?"

"Providing you always do what I tell you."

"What are the odds on that?"

"Extremely low," she said cheerfully.

"I wish you were here right now," he said. "I'd take you to bed. Show you how much I like you."

Her heart was triphammering in her breast. "Obscene phone calls are illegal."

"Chicken."

"Yep. But Seth, at Meadowland we won't—"

"Then I'll have to inveigle you to my brownstone. My bedroom has skylights and French doors onto a roof garden."

"Does it have a bed?"

"You do go for the essentials. When should I arrive on the weekend?"

"I won't be able to spend much time with you," she said hurriedly, "I have to practice for the recording sessions."

"That's fine," he said equably. "What time?"

"How about Saturday morning? As early as you like."

He was supposed to be in Texas on Saturday morning. "Nine-thirty," he said promptly.

"The coffee'll be on." Her voice suddenly faltered. "I hope...I mean, I wish...darn it, I don't know what I mean."

He felt precisely the same way. Although he, unlike her, wasn't about to admit it. "I'll see you Saturday," he said and put down the receiver.

How could one woman and one small girl make him feel so ludicrously unsettled?

Dammit, he was still in control of his life.

Scowling, he cut Paganini off in the middle of the adagio and substituted Louis Armstrong. First thing Monday morning he'd get on the phone to Texas.

By two o'clock on Saturday afternoon, Seth was beginning to wonder why he'd come. Meadowland was beautiful, a beguiling combination of unkempt woodland and wild gardens, the house itself welcoming, comfortable and pleasantly cluttered. It was the nanny's weekend off; Lia had greeted him at the door, holding a mug of coffee in front of her like a bulwark. She looked strained and tired, he thought, and forbore to say so.

Marise was polite and as far away as the rain forests of Borneo. As difficult to reach, too, Seth thought, striving to hit the delicate balance between showing her he cared, without pushing her too hard. Then, as he was sitting out on the patio in the afternoon sun, he overheard his daughter's raised voice from an open window overhead. "But I want to go for a swim, Mum."

"I can't stop yet, Marise—I've got the rest of the sonata to go through."

Sulkily Marise said, "You'll be forever."

"No, I won't. I'll be another hour."

"An hour's forever."

"Why don't you ask your father if he'll go for a swim with you?"

"I bet he doesn't have a swimsuit."

"Ask him."

"I don't want to!"

Lia sighed. "Then you'll have to wait for me."

Five minutes later, one of the French doors opened behind Seth. Marise trailed across the slate patio stones toward him. He looked up and smiled at her. "Hi, there. What's up?"

She was industriously chewing on her bottom lip. "Do you want to go for a swim?" she mumbled.

"Love to. Give me a couple of minutes to change—why don't I meet you out here?"

Her face had lightened perceptibly. "Neat."

He ran upstairs, wondering if he was a fool to regard Marise's request as a small victory. Throwing on a T-shirt and his blue trunks, he went back to the patio. She was already there, wearing a bright pink swimsuit and laden with an assortment of inflated toys. "Let's go," he said.

He unlocked the gate to the pool, threw his towel over the chair and peeled off his shirt. "Last one in's a rotten egg," he said. "Or don't kids say that anymore?"

But Marise was gazing in fascination at his chest. "Who did that to you?"

The scar over his ribs was still an angry red furrow. "I—it was an accident."

"Sometimes Suzy and I watch cowboy movies. Did a bad guy shoot you?"

"Yeah…he did."

"Was there a stagecoach?"

Seth sat down on the edge of the pool and patted the cement beside him. "It was in Africa."

"Wow," she said, "were there lions?"

Striving to censor the truth yet hold her interest, Seth began to talk. She kept interrupting him with questions, her little feet splashing in the pool, and gradually Seth shifted into telling her about some of the children he'd met on his third world trips. She edged a little closer to him, laughing at some of his jokes, big-eyed when he did describe a near-encounter with a lion, and how he'd once followed a small herd of elephants. She said with a contented sigh, "You tell good stories."

Feeling as though he'd been awarded the Nobel Prize, Seth said, "Lots more where those came from. Should we go for a swim now?"

"I can show you my backstroke," she said with a shy smile.

"I'd like that," he said with huge understatement, and slid into the water.

From the upstairs window, where she'd been trying to concentrate on a Beethoven sonata, Lia watched father and daughter cavorting in the water. She'd also watched them sitting side by side talking to each other, Seth's blond head bending to Marise's brown curls, Marise's face lifted confidingly to Seth's.

Change, Lia thought. So much change.

Seth and Marise were beginning to forge a relationship. She was happy about that, of course she was. But she wasn't blind to the consequences. Her daughter would, from now on, be shared between herself and Seth.

Don't be an idiot, Lia scolded herself. You already share Marise with Nancy; and love isn't something to be measured out in small doses.

If only Seth weren't so barricaded, so guarded. Sometimes it seemed to her that only in bed was he truly himself.

It had been a long time since he'd held her in his arms.

Seth had hauled himself out of the pool, swiping his soaked hair out of his eyes. As the sun gleamed along the long line of his spine, Lia felt desire uncurl in her belly and lazily stretch its limbs. Then he reached down and lifted Marise out of the water, carefully putting her down beside him. She was laughing at something he'd said.

Father and daughter, side by side. Grabbing a tissue, Lia wiped her eyes and turned away from the window. The score was a blur of black notes. How was she supposed to work when her world kept shifting beneath her feet?

She did work for another couple of hours, partly to give Seth and Marise more time together. After hanging up her violin, Lia went downstairs and the three of them had dinner together, then watched The Lion King on video. When it was over, Lia said, "Bedtime, honeybunch."

Marise said craftily, "You could both read me a story."

"I'll read one chapter and your father another," Lia said firmly.

Which is what they did, in Marise's pretty yellow bedroom. Seth read his way steadily through his part of the story, keeping his eyes on the page; he was finding his participation in an obviously much-loved ritual almost unbearably moving. When it was time to say good night, he contented himself with patting Marise on the shoulder. "I'll see you tomorrow," he said.

"We could go and see Suzy," Marise said, giving a little bounce on the bed. "She thinks it's awesome that you're here."

"I'd like that. Night, Marise…I had a great time with you today."

Leaving Lia to kiss Marise good night, he ran downstairs, grabbed a jacket and hurried outdoors. The stars looked very close. New leaves were rustling gently in the breeze. His mother hadn't believed in coddling her only son, and he couldn't imagine her sitting on his bed and reading about the adventures of a mouse called Stuart Little. His throat felt clogged; his shoulder muscles were tightly bunched.

As a boy, he'd been surrounded by money and the things money could buy. But Marise was by far the richer.

Seth set off down the driveway, walking fast. Too much had happened today; not the least of which had been spending several hours at Lia's beloved Meadowland. All day, with one part of his brain, he'd been achingly aware of her nearness.

It was going to half-kill him to sleep alone in the guest bedroom under the eaves.

Half an hour later, he headed back to the house. Its lights shone gold through the lacy network of branches. It would suit him just fine if Lia had already gone to bed; he'd had enough emotion for one day. He didn't need to add sexual frustration to the list.

As he went in the front door, Lia called to him from the kitchen. Reluctantly he crossed the hall. She was standing by the stove, in faded jeans and a baggy blue sweater, her hair tied back with a ribbon. "I made hot chocolate—want some?" she offered.

"Think I'll pass, and head upstairs—it's been a long day."

She put down her mug and in a low voice said, "Will you come to bed with me?"

As had so often happened, she'd rocked him to the roots. "That's not in the cards—not with Marise here."

"She's sound asleep and I'll lock my bedroom door."

He raked his fingers through his hair. "What's up, Lia?"

"Please, Seth…come to bed. We can talk there."

She still looked tired, her mouth a vulnerable curve, her eyes full of uncertainty. Any opposition he might have felt melted away. "I locked the front door," he said matter-of-factly.

She switched out the kitchen light; from upstairs, the hall light beckoned. She headed for the stairs, aware in every nerve of Seth padding behind her. She'd lit two candles in her bedroom; as she closed the door behind him, shadows flickered over his face. She had no idea what she was going to do next.

Seth put his arms around her, drew her close and pressed her face to his chest. She leaned against him. His body heat seeped through his cotton shirt; the heavy stroke of his heart felt immensely comforting, and slowly all the accumulated tensions of the day slid away. "Where's your nightgown?" he asked.

"Under the pillow."

He edged her over to the bed. His face intent, he slowly undressed her, his fingers lingering on the slope of her shoulders and the lift of her breasts, smoothing the long curve of hip and thigh as he drew her jeans down her legs; and all without saying a word. Finally he slipped her white silk gown over her head.

Her whole body felt liquid; she swayed toward him. But Seth was in no hurry. He took off his own shirt and jeans, tossing them on the rattan rocker. Then he drew her down on the bed beside him. Only then did he kiss her, a lingering kiss with none of the frantic hunger of their other couplings.

Catching his mood, Lia edged one thigh over his, linked her arms around his neck and surrendered. Slowly and surely he drew her deeper and deeper into a place lit with golden sunlight rather than with the whip of fire. Heat, yes, that melted her bones and bathed her in intimacy. A warm light that dazzled her. But instead of being caught up in a desperate drive to completion, she was surrounded by caring and sensitivity. By gentleness, she thought in wonderment.

Engulfed in the slow, sure currents of yearning, she sighed his name, her lips buried in his shoulder, then moving to caress the hard curve of his ribs. She twisted gracefully in his arms, her breasts to the tautness of his belly, and felt him slip inside her, silky and hard.

As she made a small sound of delight, Seth began to move with long, slow strokes. She moaned softly, her hips moving with him. His eyes were trained on her, molten with what she could only call tenderness. Like the green leaves of spring, she thought. Tender, vulnerable, opening to a new life.

Her heart opened in response even as her body gathered to its crescendo. Her breath was rapid in her throat, her hips pumping to bring him closer and closer; yet still her gaze held his. His own eyes had darkened to a forest-green; the thud of his heartbeat was like a primitive drumming. Caught in its rhythm, she rushed toward him, her tiny cries like the echoes of faraway music. He groaned deep in his chest. Together they fell, entwined as one.

Lia lay very still. Her cheek was pressed to his breastbone, his arms wrapped around her as though he never wanted to let her go. Like the slow unfolding of a leaf, emotion filled her heart. I'm falling in love with you, she thought. Oh, Seth, I'm falling in love…

She closed her eyes, and knew her own words for the truth. For now they were enough; and too new to be shared. Feeling utterly peaceful, she let herself drift off to sleep.

CHAPTER TWELVE

SETH had to leave right after lunch on Sunday, to prepare for a business trip to Venezuela. Marise unaffectedly hugged him goodbye, then skipped off to play in the shrubbery. Lia, tongue-tied, watched him put his leather overnight bag into the back seat of his red Porsche.

She hadn't told him she loved him; the thought terrified her. But when would she see him again? "That's a very jazzy car," she said.

He straightened and grinned at her. "You can drive it. Anytime."

"Flat out?"

"It's the only way. I've got a suggestion, Lia. Why don't you stay at my place this week while you're doing the recording? I'm away until Saturday, you'd have free run of the place."

She could see where he lived: perhaps learn more about the guarded man she'd fallen in love with. "I'd like that."

He hadn't expected her to agree so readily. Giving her the extra key, he said, "Make yourself at home. Perhaps Marise could come up next weekend?"

"Sure."

He might as well push his advantage. "My father would really like to meet her."

Lia's eyes clouded. "Your father lives with your mother. I don't want your mother anywhere near Marise."

"I'm not suggesting you invite my mother."

"I'll see," Lia said, her lips set mutinously.

Seth scribbled Allan's personal number on his card. "My father wants to mend, not to destroy," he said, lifting his hand and tracing the smooth hollow under her cheekbone. "If Marise weren't cavorting in the forsythia bushes, I'd be kissing you blind. See you Saturday—late afternoon."

He put the car in gear, beat a tattoo on the horn for his daughter's benefit, and drove away.

Six days passed, four of which Seth spent in the Venezuelan oilfields, with a side trip to Peru to check on a project his foundation had started in Lima two years ago. He was glad to get home, he thought, as he climbed the steps of his brownstone near Central Park. Everything looked the same: the polished brass door handle, the elegantly proportioned windows and the dark oak door. But inside, he knew, Lia and Marise were waiting for him.

He hadn't talked to Lia since he'd left Meadowland; since a lovemaking so different in quality that it had both disarmed and dismayed him.

Too emotional. That was the catch. The e-word, he thought with a rueful smile, unlocked the door and stepped inside. But the first person he saw wasn't Lia or Marise. It was Allan, his father, who came around the corner, his shirt rumpled and far from clean. "Seth!" he exclaimed. "We weren't expecting you for another hour."

So Lia had invited his father, Seth thought in a rush of gratitude mingled with another, deeper emotion he didn't want to name.

"Plane was early," he said prosaically. "How are you, Father?"

Allan gave him an atypically boyish grin. "Wonderful," he

said. "I've spent the day with Lia and my totally charming granddaughter—took her on a tour of my favorite bookstore. She talked the ears off me."

Seth blinked. "What's that on your shirt?"

Allan glanced down. "Fingerpaint," he said. "We're in the kitchen, why don't you join us?"

"Lia's there, too?"

"She's a lovely woman, Seth."

Seth grunted something indecipherable and followed his father into the ultramodern kitchen. The granite counters were covered with sheets of paper that had been smeared in every shade from pink to bilious green. The warm odor of chocolate chip cookies filled the air. Marise looked up. "Hi!" she crowed. "Come see my painting, can you guess what it is?"

"Mmm…an orchid?" Seth hazarded.

She giggled. "It's a flamingo—look, here are its wings."

"Ah," he said, "I see. Hello, Lia."

She was standing by the counter, wearing a T-shirt that under a riot of musical notes announced that Musicians Score. As always, he was struck first by her beauty. The shiny fall of her hair, the luscious curves of her cheekbones, now delicately flushed…had he forgotten anything about her?

"Can I have a cookie?" he asked.

Laughing, she passed the plate. "You sure can."

Effortlessly he was incorporated into the chatter and warmth. If Allan looked different, so too did his own house, Seth realized. Cluttered. Lived in. In a way that he'd never managed on his own.

A family kind of clutter.

He kept this thought to himself.

An hour later, they walked three or four blocks to a trattoria Seth frequented; on the way, to his annoyance, they ran into a media crew conducting a survey. Although Marise was entranced by the cameras and questions, Seth hurried her past them. "I'm starving," he said. "The last time I ate was in Miami. Did I tell you about the dog at the airport?"

Deflected, Marise skipped along beside him. "Was it a Dalmatian?"

"It was a Scottie with very short legs," he said, and took her by the hand to cross the street.

"Is it another story?" she asked hopefully.

"I believe it might be."

"I like the way you tell stories," Marise said. "What am I s'posed to call you?"

Seth stopped dead in the middle of the street. "You could try Dad. If you felt like it. Or Seth is fine with me."

"Dad's best. What happened to the Scottie?"

He tried to gather his wits; her small hand curled in his, her astonishing acceptance of him as her father, had thrown him for a loop. "We're nearly at the restaurant," he said. "Why don't I save it until we're sitting down?"

Allan went ahead with her; Seth turned to Lia, realizing how quiet she'd been. He said softly, his hand at the small of her back, "How are you?"

"I missed you," Lia said. It was true. She had missed him, unrelentingly, day and night. She'd also, when she'd seen Marise hold his hand a few minutes ago, fallen a little more deeply in love with him.

"I'd like to be making love with you right now," Seth said.

"That, too," she said, tossing her head.

"So why else did you miss me?" he rapped, his smile fading.

"I'll tell you later," she said and walked across the charming patio of the trattoria to one of the brightly painted tables.

Yes, he thought, you will, and sat down at the table. But that evening, once Marise was settled in bed, Allan said edgily, "Seth, can I have a word with you? In private."

Lia stood up, stretching lazily. "I'm going to have a leisurely bath and go to bed early," she said. "I'll see you both in the morning."

She was avoiding him, Seth thought. Had been ever since he'd arrived home. What was going on? Not that he was likely to find out with all these people around.

Trying to tamp down his frustration, he watched her leave the room. He needed to touch her. Hold her in his arms. That way he'd find out what the matter was.

Meanwhile Allan was pacing up and down the faded antique carpet. As soon as Lia shut the door behind her, he said jerkily, "I've left your mother."

"What?"

"She was furious that I was planning to come to Manhattan to see Marise. Absolutely furious. Forbade me to even think of it. One thing led to another…and for the first time in years I didn't back down, Seth. I held my ground."

"Good for you," Seth said warmly.

"She told me if I came to Manhattan today, she'd never speak to me again. So I said she was right, she wouldn't, because I wouldn't be living with her anymore…I've moved into a suite at the Ritz-Carlton." His smile was wry. "To say she was taken aback is putting it mildly."

"I'm proud of you, Dad," Seth said, noticing absently how easily the diminutive slipped off his tongue.

"Thanks, son," Allan said huskily. "She's not an easy woman, your mother. But I've never told you about her background—she didn't want anyone to know, least of all you, so she swore me to secrecy years ago. Now that I've left her, I don't feel bound by that promise any longer…she had a terrible childhood, Seth. Unrelenting poverty coupled with violence. Her father was a migrant worker, and when he hit the bottle, which was frequently, he also took out the belt and hit whichever kid was nearest—she ran away from home when she was fourteen, got herself a menial job and never saw him again. Never trusted anyone again, as far as I can tell. Even me, who loves her. But for the sake of that skinny little girl picking grapes when she should have been in school, I've forgiven her a great deal."

Shaken, Seth said, "I didn't know any of that."

"Maybe I should have told you long ago, despite Eleonore's wishes to the contrary. But somehow the occasion never arose."

Seth asked several questions, learning more about his parents' difficult marriage in half an hour than he had in all his thirty-seven years. Allan finished by saying heavily, "Not even for Eleonore will I shut myself off from my granddaughter. Not for anyone."

"Marise is a sweetheart."

"As is her mother."

Seth didn't want to talk about Lia. "You look tired, Dad, and I know I'm wiped. Worked my guts out all last week. Shall we hit the pit?"

"I'm glad we had this talk, son. Long overdue."

"I'm glad, too." Seth gave his father a rough hug and watched him leave the room. His head was whirling, from a combination of jet lag, information overload and too much emotion.

He craved sleep. But more than that, he craved Lia. Who was sleeping in the guest wing next to her daughter.

She might as well be in Venezuela.

Seth was up before anyone else in the morning. He went downstairs and settled himself with his coffee in the breakfast nook that overlooked the garden. As was his habit, he skimmed through the newspapers first, to get an overview of what was going on in the world.

On the seventh page of the second section was a large colored photo of himself, Lia, Marise and Allan. "Family Out-ing," the caption read, giving his and Allan's names. Lia d'Angeli was listed as Seth's companion, Marise as her daughter. His eyes and his daughter's had been printed an identical, startling green.

Companion, thought Seth, feeling his temper rise. What kind of word was that? The caption hadn't needed to say anything else. The point was made. Lia as mistress, Marise as illegitimate child.

Himself as the father who didn't care enough to put things right.

Goddammit, he wasn't going to put up with it. Vienna had been bad enough. But Vienna was on the other side of the Atlantic. New York was where he lived, the headquarters of his company. They'd hit too close to home this time.

No more.

It wasn't an opportune moment for Lia to wander into the kitchen, rubbing her eyes. She was wearing a long silk robe streaked with blues and reds, belted around her waist; her hair was a loose tangle down her back. She sniffed the air. "Coffee," she said. "You're an angel."

He said flatly, "Are the others still in bed?"

Her eyes snapped wide. "What's the matter?"

"Are they?"

"Yes. Why?"

He thrust the paper at her, jabbing at the picture with his finger. "I won't have this, Lia. I won't have Marise subjected to any more gossip and innuendo. We're going to get married and put an end to it."

She took the paper from him, reading the caption. Frowning, she said, "Marise has already told everyone at school that you're her father. So this doesn't really matter."

He surged to his feet. "It matters to me. And it should damn well matter to you."

"I've lived with the fact of my daughter's illegitimacy for

seven years," she said steadily, reaching up in the cupboard for a mug. "And don't you dare tell me how I should feel."

He snatched the mug from her and banged it on the counter. Pulling her against the length of his body, he plummeted to find her mouth. Shock made her, momentarily, rigid. Then she opened to him, digging her nails into his shoulders and kissing him back with searing passion. Flame tore through him; he cupped her breast and jammed his hips to hers.

Then, as roughly, he pushed her away. "How soon can you get married?"

"Are you asking me to marry you or telling me I'm going to marry you?"

She looked magnificent, her cheeks the same bright red as the pattern in her robe. "It's not up for negotiation," he said.

"That's what you think."

"Yes, Lia, that's what I think."

Her back to the counter, her hands clasping the smooth edge, she said, "Do you love me, Seth?"

"No."

"So how can you say we're getting married?"

"I like you, I admire and respect you, and I sure as hell lust after you. That's not a bad start."

"It's not enough."

"Then you're a starry-eyed romantic."

"Don't make fun of my feelings!"

His eyes narrowed. "What are you getting at?"

"I've fallen in love with you," she said evenly.

He opened his mouth to argue with her. But something in her stance and her clear gaze made the words die on his lips. "When did that happen?"

"I realized it the last time we made love…at Meadowland. Maybe it happened a long time ago in Paris, who knows. It doesn't really matter. The fact remains that I won't marry you if you don't love me."

"Love's the most abused word in the language."

"That's your opinion—it doesn't happen to be mine. I deserve a husband who loves me, and Marise deserves parents who love each other. End of discussion."

"My father loved my mother," Seth snarled. "Much good it's done him."

"My parents loved music, their careers, each other and me. Not necessarily in that order. We can do it all, that's what I'm trying to say."

"You're a deluded optimist."

"I'm a realist. After all, we both love Marise. That's a start—a wonderful start."

He did indeed love his daughter. "It is wonderful. But it's not the start of anything. For me it's all there is."

"I won't compromise, Seth—I want the whole nine yards," she said, her chin tilted. "A husband who loves me and who loves our child."

She wasn't playing hard to get: he knew her too well for that. So it was up to him to change her mind. Short of throwing her over his shoulder and lugging her to the nearest registry office, Seth had no idea how to begin. "Corporate mergers are a piece of cake compared to you," he said caustically.

"I should hope so," she said, her dark eyes full of defiance.

"You look as though you could chew me up for breakfast and spit me out before lunch."

"I have to have my coffee first," she answered with a glint of amusement.

Seth stepped closer, slipping his arms around her waist. Her body felt deliciously warm and soft, all voluptuous curves under thin silk. "If only we could go to bed together," he muttered.

"Sex is no substitute for love. Not in my books."

Surprising them both, he laughed. "When it's sex with you, it comes darn close."

Swiftly she reached up, fisting her hand in his hair and

dragging his head down, then hungrily sealing his lips with her own. The kiss slammed through him. Feasting on all the sweetness of her mouth, he pulled her closer.

Footsteps clattered on the stairs. Lia shoved Seth away and hurriedly straightened her robe. "It's Marise," she gasped.

Seth was in no shape to face his daughter. He turned to the counter and busied himself pouring Lia a mug of coffee. Unfinished business, he thought savagely. Welcome to fatherhood, Seth. The trouble was, Lia was going home to Meadowland tonight, then to Prague later in the week; while he was leaving for London and Malaysia first thing in the morning.

The wedding date wasn't set. She'd won this round.

CHAPTER THIRTEEN

THE cab dropped Seth off in front of Rudolfinum, the neo-Renaissance concert hall on the banks of the Vltava in Prague. It was pouring rain. He ran for the entrance, his black shoes splashing through the puddles.

He was late. He'd be lucky if he made it for the intermission.

He hadn't planned to come to Prague. He'd planned the exact opposite. To keep his distance from Lia for a while. Let her cool her heels, come to her senses and decide to marry him.

The usher led him through the well-dressed crowd mingling during the intermission to the best box in the house; Seth had achieved this by pulling any number of strings at once. The door to the box closed behind him. He hung up his raincoat and sat down in the plush seat. His trousers clung damply to his legs. His hair was wet.

But he'd made it in time to hear Lia play.

The audience as well as the orchestra were filtering back to their seats. The stage was high-arched, backed by an array of gleaming organ pipes. Seth's box was in full view of the podium. Would Lia see him?

When she was playing, her focus was too strong for her to be distracted. He hoped.

He hadn't made love to her since that night at Meadowland.

It felt like forever. Wasn't that why he was here? To make love to Lia?

He was here to change her mind on the subject of marriage.

He had a reputation as a perennial bachelor; in the early days of his career, the gossip magazines had used up considerable ink trying to pair him off with one glamorous beauty after another, all to no avail. Yet now he was determined to marry a woman he didn't love, a woman who was, moreover, resisting him every step of the way.

Did he want to marry solely for Marise's sake?

Hadn't he been avoiding this question all week?

A panel in the wall swung open and directly across from him Lia walked out on the stage. The audience broke into spontaneous clapping. As she acknowledged the applause, looking around her, she suddenly saw him.

Her steps faltered. Even from his perch, Seth could see shock flash across her face. Then it was gone, erased as though it had never been. She took her place by the podium and smiled at the conductor.

Her dress was scarlet, strapless and slim-fitting, her lips the same uncompromising color. Her hair was drawn back with two sparkling clips; with a clench in his gut Seth noticed she was wearing the earrings he'd given her. Just before the conductor raised his baton, she looked directly at Seth.

Intimate. Intense. Challenging. How would he describe that look? It had gone straight through him, he knew that much.

As she raised her instrument to her chin, the orchestra played a single chord. Then the violin began its restless, lonely searching, lyrical and melancholy. Seth sat stone-still. Although the Nielsen violin concerto had long been one of his favorites, tonight it was as though he'd never heard it before. Lia was playing for him alone, he knew she was; as the minutes passed, she released all her love, passion and pain in a glorious outpouring of music that shook him to the core.

The final chord filled the sumptuous hall. A roar of applause broke out. Feeling as though he'd been stripped naked in full view of every soul in the hall, Seth got up, left the box and sought out the house manager in his office. "Would you see that Lia d'Angeli gets this note?" he said, passing over a sealed envelope with a banknote discreetly tucked beneath it.

"Certainly, sir. My pleasure."

Seth thanked him and took a cab through the unrelenting rain back to his hotel in the Old Town. The next move was up to Lia.

Either she came to him of her own free will, or not at all.

He had a shower, changed into casual slacks and a sweater and poured himself a drink. The post-concert reception, he knew, could take a while. All he had to do was wait. When had he ever sat in a hotel room in one of the most beautiful cities in Europe and waited for a woman to come to him?

Never.

The minutes ticked by. He flicked through the channels on the TV, trying to attune his ears to the various languages, then giving up in disgust. It was nearly midnight. Shouldn't she be here by now?

The phone rang on the cherrywood desk, making him start. Seth snatched it up. "Yes?"

"It's Lia. I'm in the lobby."

"Suite 700. Take the elevator to the top floor."

"I'll be right up," Lia said and put down the phone.

But for a moment she stayed where she was, gazing blindly at the elegant Art Nouveau decor. She knew what would happen if she went to Seth's suite. Was that what she wanted? If not, why was she here? Gathering her skirts in her hand, she walked swiftly toward the elevator.

Just as she raised her fist to tap on the door of his suite, Seth opened it. Instinctively she took a step backward, and saw his jaw harden. "Lia," he said, "come in. Did you get soaked in the rain?"

"The taxi driver very kindly held his umbrella over me, and then parked under the awning of the hotel," she prattled. "He loves Dvořák, so we had lots to talk about."

"You probably made his night. Would you like a drink?"

"No, thanks. Not after what happened in Vienna."

"Were you pleased with the concert?" he asked, cursing himself for making small talk as though she were a casual acquaintance.

"Yes. Were you?"

So the small talk was over. "How could I not be," he said, "when you played only for me?"

She didn't bother denying it. "Another way of telling you I love you."

"You think I'm so thickheaded that I wouldn't realize that? I heard you. Heard love, desire and tears."

"I was pleading my case." Her red dress swishing softly as she moved, she walked closer to him, resting one hand on his sleeve. "Perhaps too strongly. But I can't make myself into another kind of woman, Seth. I am who I am. Impatient. Passionate. Uncompromising. Can you not love that woman?"

"I've never in my life fallen in love. Had no use for it."

"So I'm the same as all the rest?" she flashed.

"You're utterly different—but I can't make myself fall in love to order!"

"Won't, you mean."

"Can't is what I said."

"Then I won't marry you."

"What is this," he demanded, "a battle of wills to see who comes out on top?"

"As it stands now, we're all losers. You. Me. And Marise."

"Now you're fighting dirty," he grated.

"Did you expect any different?"

In spite of himself, he lifted one hand to trace the soft

curve of her cheek and the jut of bone above it. "I want to go to bed with you."

Unconsciously she swayed toward him. "I want that, too," she whispered.

His heart was juddering in his chest. "Suits me a lot better than arguing."

"No more words, Seth," she said with sudden fierceness. "Take me to bed. Make love to me, make me forget everything but your body."

He lifted her off her feet, carrying her across the thick carpets to his bedroom with its imposing four-poster bed; there, he laid her down on her back and flung himself on top of her, hauling his sweater over his head. "You drive me out of my mind," he muttered, then plunged to ravage her mouth. Her tongue laced with his, her teeth scraping his lip, a small pain that only served to inflame him. She was writhing beneath him, mouth and hands so hungry that he lost all restraint. Throwing himself sideways, carrying her with him, he yanked on the zipper of her dress and tugged it down the length of her body.

Her bare breasts, the slide of silk over her hips…would he ever have enough of her? She was fumbling with the clips in her hair, tossing them onto the floor so that her hair spread like dark satin on the pillow. Her irises, so dark he could lose himself in them, were blurred with desire.

Fiercely he took from her, giving no quarter, feeling her nails rake his back, her teeth nip his shoulder. She was his mate, meeting him in every way that mattered, hunger for hunger in a primitive dance. Tasting, teasing, arousing, he traveled every inch of her body, making it his own.

She was his.

But he didn't love her.

When he entered her, she arched and bucked, her fingers like manacles around his wrists. He plunged, deep, deeper, groaning her name as he fought for breath.

The climax ripped through her, leaving her breathless and spent; his whole body pounding his own release, Seth dropped his head to her shoulder, feeling sweat cool on his bare back.

He had no memory of how he'd gotten out of the rest of his clothes. Or where they were. Not that it mattered.

He turned on his side, burying his face between her breasts. This was what he wanted, Seth thought dimly. Lia in his arms. What more could there be?

He'd left Malaysia very early that morning after three days of intense meetings. With the suddenness of a small boy, Seth fell asleep.

Lia lay still, listening as Seth's breathing settled into a smooth rhythm. For the first time after making love to him, she felt less than fulfilled. Physically she was satiated; that was a given. But her soul felt empty, she thought unhappily. At the moment of climax, she'd wanted to cry out how much she loved him; and hadn't done so. He didn't want to hear those words from her, because he didn't share them.

How strange to feel lonely when Seth's arm was draped over her hip and his breath was wafting the curve of her breast. Yet lonely was how she felt.

She waited another few minutes before slipping free of his embrace. He muttered something in his sleep, reaching for her. Paralyzed, she crouched on the bed. Only when his breathing had steadied again did she scramble to the floor. There were two fleecy robes in the bathroom. Belting one around her, she went to sit in one of the window seats, upholstered in embossed brocade. The lights of Prague twinkled through the leaded panes. Like diamonds on black velvet, she thought, fingering the earrings Seth had given her.

A church spire lanced the darkness. Several streets over, the river wound its lazy way through a city where she'd always felt at home, so permeated was it with music.

But now she felt exiled. In playing for Seth, she'd given

him her heart; yet she'd failed to reach him, or to change him. Dropping her head to her knees, Lia let the slow tears course down her cheeks.

She wept in silence until she was drained of emotion. Getting up, she went to the bathroom, washed her face and walked slowly back to the bedroom. Her dress was lying in a crumpled heap on the floor. Red as blood, she thought with a superstitious shiver, and picked it up. Her underwear was on Seth's side of the bed, tangled in his trousers. Moving as quietly as she could, she got dressed.

But as she reached for the cold sparkle of her hair clips, she bumped the side of the bed. Seth stirred. "Lia?" he muttered. "What are you doing?"

Frozen to the spot, she watched him rear up on one elbow. He reached for the bedside lamp and switched it on. Blinking in the light, she said, "I'm going back to my hotel."

He swung his legs over the side of the bed, running his fingers through his tousled hair; he was instantly awake in a way that frightened her. "You're running away," he said. "Just as you did in Paris."

"It's too late for that," she said bitterly. "Because of Marise, I'm tied to you." She dropped the clip into her evening bag. "I have to fly to Basel in the morning—a final concert before I go home."

"Why are you leaving now, in the middle of the night?"

The truth, she thought. Why not tell the truth? "I can't do this," she said, despair thinning her voice. "I love you. To be with you like this, knowing you don't love me—it's too painful. It tears me apart."

"You came to my hotel. Knowing what would happen."

"I didn't know how I'd feel afterward—how could I? Tell me, Seth, why did you come to the concert?"

"I couldn't stay away. I needed to touch you, hold you in my arms. It nearly drove me crazy having you stay in my house last weekend, knowing I couldn't take you to bed. Couldn't even kiss you the way I wanted to."

. "There's more to making love than the physical," Lia cried. "Do you know how I felt tonight? Why I couldn't go to sleep? I was lonely. Horribly, desperately lonely. I can't separate making love with you from being in love with you. It's that simple. And that complicated."

He said in an ugly voice, "So if I don't fall in love with you, I don't get to go to bed with you?"

"You make it sound like I'm blackmailing you! I'm just trying to protect myself."

He stood up and walked over to her, unselfconscious in his nudity. "Come to bed with me now, Lia...you need to sleep. I don't know what we're going to do any more than you do. But surely we can work something out."

His body, as well-known to her as her own, towered over her, pulling her to him as effortlessly as a magnet attracts metal. "I can't, Seth," she whispered. "It hurts too much. You're giving me all the gifts of your body—but you're holding the rest back."

"I'm not holding anything back—it's not there to give."

His words were like a death knell. "I'll stay out of your way when you come to Meadowland to see Marise," Lia said tonelessly, "and Nancy can deliver her when she goes to Manhattan to stay with you."

"Marise is a highly intelligent child. You think we can behave like a couple of strangers without her noticing? You told me she deserves parents who love each other. I'm not so ambitious—as far as I'm concerned, she deserves parents who can be in the same room together."

"Stop!" Lia exclaimed, covering her ears. "I'll do the best I can, for Marise's sake—I promise."

"Then marry me," Seth said harshly.

Knowing she had to get out of here, Lia said nastily, "I see how you got to the top—you're ruthless, you don't care about other people's feelings. I'll clear it with Nancy when I get home, and you and Marise can work out how often you want to see each other. Dammit, where's my other shoe?"

"Under the bed," he said, bending to retrieve it, then passing it to her.

She took it gingerly and shoved her foot into it. "Good night. Sleep well."

She looked like a firecracker about to explode. She also looked like a woman on the edge. "Lia," he said hoarsely, "I can't help the way I was brought up. That night when I overheard my mother telling Dad about the abortion—it killed something inside me. The ability to love. I can't give myself to a woman, it isn't in me."

Her eyes were dark as woodland pools. "You're saying I should take you as you are?"

Grateful for her understanding, Seth said, "Yeah, I guess that's what I'm saying. I'll be faithful to you, I'll be the best father to Marise that I can possibly be...but that's as far as it goes."

She remembered how her violin had wandered through a desert of notes, searching for a place to rest, only finding it after long struggle; and shook her head. "You already love Marise. Your father and you are mending years of neglect." Her lips curved gently. "And you love music. How can you say you're unable to love?"

He didn't smile back. "I'm talking about you, not Marise or my father. I've lived with myself for a long time—I should know by now what I'm capable of."

He looked so adamant. So unmovable. "You're letting fear run your life," Lia accused.

Flicked on the raw, Seth said, "I wish it was as simple as that. It's not. It's a blankness—an emptiness. A lack. Hell, I don't even know how to describe it."

"So tell me about it," Lia said fiercely. "Make me understand."

Why not tell her? What did he have to lose? Seth sat down on the edge of the bed. "I was eight years old, a year older than Marise. I'd sneaked down to the library that night to get a book—I used to read in bed till all hours—when I heard my father coming, and hid behind the big leather couch. He sat down at his desk and started going through some bills. Then my mother came down the hall, talking to one of the servants. Dad called her in and held out a piece of paper, asking what she'd had done at the private clinic she always went to."

He paused, lost in memory. His mother had been wearing a black cashmere sweater and a strand of pearls; as a boy, he'd thought it was weird that a pearl could come out of an oyster. "She said she'd had an abortion," he went on, ironing any emotion from his voice. "I'll never forget the shock on my father's face. He asked if there'd been a medical reason. No, she said, she simply didn't want another child. Then my father asked if it had been a boy or a girl. A girl, she said indifferently, as though she was talking about a dress she'd discarded. My father was crying, tears sliding down his face—it terrified me. *A daughter,* he said. *Eleonore, you know I've always wanted a daughter.*"

Seth rubbed his jaw, trying to lessen the tension. "I didn't know what abortion meant, but I knew my mother had done something terrible. Then my father said, *How could you have done that?* My mother rarely lost her temper, control was too important to her. But she lost it then, screamed at my father that she'd never bring a little girl into the world, threw a priceless crystal statue at one of the cabinets—there were shards of glass everywhere—and stormed out of the library. Eventually my father got up, staggering like an old man…he went down the hall and I heard his bedroom door close. That's when I ran upstairs to bed."

"Seth, that's a terrible story," Lia faltered. She reached out her arms, her one urge to comfort the little boy he'd been and the man he'd become.

He struck them down. "Don't," he said in a voice scraped raw, that long-ago dissonance of terror and incomprehension swirling in his head. "This wasn't a bid for sympathy."

"I didn't think it was." Lia made one last try, letting the words pour out. "Seth, I talked to your father last weekend—on Sunday, after you'd left. He told me a little about your mother's upbringing, how violent it was. Despite my parents' careers, I had such a happy childhood, filled with music and the constant undercurrent of knowing I was loved. I can't imagine a childhood like Eleonore's. It made me understand her a little—perhaps even begin to forgive her for the harm she did to me. Couldn't you do the same?"

"Forgiveness isn't the issue. I wanted you to understand why I'm not into marriage, that's all. My father loved my mother. He gave her his soul and she trampled all over it. So I learned very young that love means betrayal and heartbreak."

"It doesn't have to!"

"A barrier slammed down that night, against knowledge I was too young to comprehend and emotions too terrible to bear. It's still in place. It always will be."

It was the finality in Seth's voice that destroyed Lia's last vestige of hope. Her whole body felt ice-cold. Picking up her wrap, she clumsily drew it around her shoulders. "Thank you for telling me," she said helplessly. "I'd better go…I'll see myself out."

Seth made no move to stop her. Feeling as though her own heart was breaking, Lia hurried out of the bedroom.

CHAPTER FOURTEEN

SUMMER had arrived at Meadowland. The flower beds were a riot of color, birds were nesting in the trees and the swimming pool shone turquoise in the sunshine as Lia and Marise frolicked in the deep end.

Lia should have been happy. Marise was out of school. She herself had only two summer festivals to attend and a benefit concert at Carnegie Hall; so she was able to spend hours of precious time with her daughter. The vegetable garden was flourishing and they had a bumper crop of strawberries.

Marise had spent a lot of time with Seth; he'd gone to her school closing, and the last three weekends had taken her to his summer home on Cape Cod, where he'd introduced her to sailing and ocean swimming. He'd also dropped in at Meadowland twice with Allan, occasions that had sorely tested Lia's composure.

Not once had he mentioned marriage; it was as though he'd forgotten both his proposal and her refusal. Certainly he never mentioned the night a little boy had hidden in the library of the big stone house by the sea. Instead he treated her with a courtesy that scoured every nerve in her body; he might as well have been in Paris as standing in her sun-dappled kitchen.

Marise loved him, and he loved Marise. That much, she knew.

He'd never love herself. She knew that, too; and ached every moment of the day from the knowledge.

Marise splashed her. "Mum, watch me dive all the way to the bottom! Dad taught me how."

With a start Lia came back to the present, to her daughter heaving her lungs full of air, then kicking herself deeper and deeper into the water. When Marise surfaced a few moments later, red-faced and sputtering, Lia said, "Great, Marise—you're a way better swimmer than last year."

"Dad's teaching me all kinds of neat things." Marise put her head to one side, trying to get water out of her ear. "Why don't you ever come to Cape Cod with us?"

Lia should have been prepared for this question; and wasn't. "It's better that you make your own relationship with your father, Marise." She sounded like a self-help book, she thought in disgust.

"Hasn't he asked you?"

"He has a lot of catching up to do…seven years, honey-bunch. You don't need me around for that."

Marise's chin, so like her mother's, had a stubborn tilt. "You'd like his house in Cape Cod. There's two kids next door for me to play with…I'm going to ask him to ask you next time."

"You mustn't!" Lia gasped, swallowing a mouthful of chlorinated water.

"He said I could ask him anything I liked."

Cursing Seth inwardly, Lia said weakly, "This is different."

Marise was batting at the water with her fingers; her eyes looked more turquoise than green. She said in a rush, "I wish you and Dad would live together. All the time."

"Oh, Marise…"

"You could get married." Marise's smile was artless. "In the garden. I could be the bridesmaid. There's lots of flowers out now, you wouldn't even have to buy a bouquet."

Lia bit her lip. "Sweetheart, it isn't that simple."

"I don't see why not. Dad's really nice," Marise pleaded, a catch in her voice. "He could live here—he likes it here, he said so."

Lia stared at her daughter, one word overriding all the rest of the words tumbling in her brain. Selfish, she thought. She'd been utterly selfish the past few weeks. Acting as though marrying Seth only affected her.

Marise now had two parents, something she'd always longed for. Why wouldn't she want her parents safely married? Most of her school friends had a mother and a father who lived in the same house, slept in the same bed, came together to parent-teacher interviews. Ordinary. Normal. Of course Marise wanted the same.

Lia said with attempted briskness, "I promise I'll think about everything you've said, sweetie. Now we'd better get out and get dried off. I want to make strawberry jam before supper."

"Okay." Marise gave a gap-toothed grin. "I'll beat you to the end of the pool. Then I can help hull the berries."

By nine o'clock that night Marise was sound asleep in bed, her fingers still red-stained, and Lia was standing in the kitchen gazing at the neat row of jars filled with ruby-red jam. They'd taste wonderful in February, she thought absently. What in heaven's name was she going to do?

Behind her, the phone shrilled. The number that came up was Seth's. With a superstitious shiver Lia picked up the receiver and said hello.

"Lia. How are you?"

Confused. Unhappy. Terrified. "Fine," she said.

"I wondered if I could pick Marise up tomorrow morning? She's been asking to go to the IMAX, and there's a show on tomorrow evening about whales. I could bring her back the next day."

"Sure," Lia said. "Come early, she'll want you to have a tour of the garden."

"See you around ten, then."

She opened her mouth to say she needed to talk to him, but the connection was already cut. Saying a very rude word, Lia slammed the receiver back in its cradle and wiped the sticky spots of jam off the counter. Nancy was on holiday. Quickly, before she could change her mind, she picked up the phone and arranged to have Marise play with Suzy tomorrow morning until about eleven.

That way, she'd be alone with Seth.

But only for an hour.

The traffic was worse than Seth had anticipated, and it was 10:25 before he turned into the long driveway to Meadowland. As always, its serenity tugged at his heart. Lia couldn't have chosen a better place to bring up Marise, he thought, and steeled himself for the inevitable meeting with Lia.

He hated them. He spent every one of them being painstakingly polite to her, when all he really wanted was to kiss her senseless.

He couldn't do that. Not in front of his seven-year-old daughter.

He parked by the front door, ran up the steps, knocked on the screen door and let himself in. "Marise?" he called. "Are you ready?"

Lia walked out into the pool of sunshine on the worn pine floor. "Hello, Seth."

She was wearing yellow shorts and a loose white shirt, her hair in a ponytail; her feet were bare, her toenails painted neon-orange. Her slender legs, delicately tanned, made his head swim. Then his heart gave a nasty jolt in his chest as he noticed how tense she looked. Tense, guarded and unhappy. "What's wrong?" he demanded. "Where's Marise?"

"I sent her over to Suzy's for a few minutes. I need to talk to you."

His pulse was now thudding in his ears. "Is she all right?"

"Yes...I've made coffee. Come in the kitchen."

The windows were open, the curtains flapping lazily in the breeze. "What's up, Lia?"

She poured his coffee, indicating the cream and sugar on the counter. "If you still want me to, I'll marry you."

This time, his heart gave an actual lurch in his rib cage. "You'll what?"

"You heard."

She was standing braced against the counter, her arms folded over her chest. Keeping his own distance, Seth said carefully, "What made you change your mind?"

"Marise. She really wants us to get married. She wants a normal life, Seth—two parents under the same roof. It was selfish of me to think only of my own needs, blinding myself to hers."

Seth said, even more carefully, "Are you still in love with me?"

"Of course. It's the forever kind of love and I'm stuck with it."

There was as much emotion in her voice as if she was discussing the grocery list. Feeling the first twinge of anger, Seth said, "If it weren't for Marise, you wouldn't be marrying me."

"You got it."

She was now gazing out the window as though he wasn't even there. Her face, normally so expressive, looked blank. As if she'd gone into hiding, he thought, unease adding itself to anger. "How soon do you want to get married?" he asked, keeping his eyes trained on her.

"As soon as possible. There's no reason to procrastinate."

"You sound so cold-blooded," he burst out.

"You're the one who started this farcical idea of marrying me to stop the gossip."

"But now it's segued into giving Marise what she needs." He hesitated, knowing he was on the brink of a momentous decision, wondering if he was making a disastrous mistake. "Why don't we try for two weeks from now? Does that fit your schedule?"

"I'm playing at Carnegie next week. Otherwise I'm free until early August."

He could shift his trip to Australia to later in the month. "Do you want a big wedding?"

"No!" she said, looking hunted. "A small one. Here."

"We have to let the media know. Or else we're defeating the purpose," Seth said sharply.

"Afterward. We'll let them know afterward."

"This is all wrong, Lia—we sound like we're planning a funeral, not a wedding."

She shrank away from him. "I don't know how else to do it."

"When we tell Marise, you could try looking happy at the prospect of marrying me," he said with brutal truth.

But even that didn't rouse her. "I will," she said. "I'll look after my end of it, and you look after yours."

He wanted her fighting him, he realized with a cold thunk in his chest. The old Lia, fiery-tempered, not giving an inch. Eyes glittering, face lit with passion.

That's what he wanted. And that's what he wasn't going to get. He said, sounding like a robot, "We'll sleep together after we're married. That's nonnegotiable."

"Naturally. Marise is quite old enough to know that Suzy's mum and dad sleep in the same room."

So once again he was back to Marise. "I'll see about getting the license."

"I'll ask the minister of our local church to do the ceremony. Do you want a ring?"

"Yes," he said, "I do. What about you?"

"I guess so. It'd look better."

"So this wedding is all about appearances."

"Well, isn't it?"

He said flatly, "I think I hear Marise."

Through the open window he'd heard someone dump a bicycle on the porch. As the screen door slammed shut, he watched Lia gather herself: as though she were about to play in a concert, she was going inward, he thought, connecting to all her resources. Then Marise came running into the kitchen. "Hi, Dad!" she crowed and flung herself at him.

He swung her up and over his head, laughing at her, wondering if he'd ever get over the wonder of her existence. "Hi, there. Ready for the movie?"

"All my clothes are packed, and Robert."

Robert was the large, rather dilapidated bear that traveled everywhere with her. "Good. I've told your mother I'll bring you home tomorrow afternoon."

Lia said easily, "Marise, we have some news for you. Big news that we hope will make you very happy." As she glanced over at Seth, she was smiling. "Why don't I tell her, Seth?"

He tried to loosen the tension in his jaw. "Go ahead."

"We're going to be married, Marise. Your father and I."

Marise looked from one to the other of them, her eyes huge. "Will Dad live with us?"

Finally Seth found his voice. "Sometimes I have to travel for work, just as your mother does, and sometimes we could spend weekends in Manhattan. But most of the time, I'll be living here."

"Like a real dad?"

"I'll do my best," he pledged, his throat tight.

Marise threw her arms around her mother. "I won't mind sharing you. Not with Dad."

There were tears sparkling on Lia's lashes. Suddenly tired of pretense, Seth put his arm around her, pulling her close. "We could get married in the garden," he said.

"Can Suzy come?" Marise asked.

"It'll be a small wedding," Lia said, giving Seth another of those brilliant, fake smiles.

"It'll be perfect," Marise warbled and started dancing around the kitchen. "Why don't you come with us to the movies, Mum?"

Seth felt a tiny shudder travel the length of Lia's body. She said calmly, "I have to practice for the Carnegie concert, sweetie. Maybe next time...you should get on your way. I packed a few sandwiches, Seth, and some juice."

"Thanks," he said. "Want to put them in the car, Marise?"

As his daughter skipped out of the kitchen, he turned Lia in his arms, ignoring her resistance, and kissed her full on the mouth in an impressive mixture of anger, frustration and desire. "There," he said, "that feels better."

She'd been rigid in his embrace. He added, baring his teeth in a smile, "I'll tell you one thing—it won't be boring, being married to you."

Then he strode out of the kitchen to join his daughter.

Four days later, Seth was one of the crowd taking their seats in Carnegie Hall. This time he wasn't in a tuxedo heading for an exclusive box seat; he was in casual clothes, sitting quite far back and to one side on the parquet level, along with a thousand other listeners.

He didn't want Lia to see him.

Above his head shone the circle of lights that memorialized the wedding band Andrew Carnegie had given his wife. An ironic touch, Seth thought, with his own wedding due to happen in just over a week.

He hadn't gone to bed with Lia since the night in Prague; he'd invited her back to his brownstone tonight, but she'd refused. She was icily polite with him when they were alone, and overly animated when Marise was around. He wasn't sure which he disliked more. But if his fiery, argumentative

Lia were to return, she wouldn't be marrying him. He couldn't have it both ways.

He'd gotten what he wanted, at the cost of driving Lia underground to a place where she was unreachable: he felt a million miles away from the woman who would be his wife in less than ten days. Was this why he was here, to try to reconnect with her in some way?

Pretty pathetic, he thought, and settled in his red plush seat to read the program.

Last night had been even more pathetic. Unable to sleep, he'd prowled around the house from midnight to three in the morning, rearranging books that didn't need rearranging, doing a wash that could have waited another day. Running from his own questions.

Why couldn't he fall in love with Lia?

That was the only question that mattered. To which he always came up with the same answer: the barrier that had slammed down when he was eight was firmly locked in place.

He was still behind it, Seth thought as the orchestra tuned up; and it was from behind it that he watched his beautiful Lia.

She wasn't his. Not really.

Because he didn't love her.

As she walked onstage in a shimmer of black silk, Seth forced himself to pay attention. But at the intermission, he got up and left the massive brown brick building on the corner of 7th Avenue. Thrusting his hands in his pockets, he walked east on 57th, then north on Madison toward his brownstone.

Lia had made at least three mistakes in the first movement of the concerto; although she'd recovered each time with lightning speed, he knew the critics would savage her the next day.

He felt responsible. Him and his ultimatum.

But how could they call off the wedding? Marise would be devastated.

He let himself indoors and ran upstairs, hoping against

hope that Lia might have left a message on his machine during the intermission. She hadn't. And although he stayed up until well past two, she didn't contact him. He even got up early the next morning, praying that she'd share with him her feelings about two very lukewarm reviews.

At nine-thirty, when Seth was getting out of the shower, the doorbell rang. He dragged on a pair of jeans, tried to subdue his wet hair and took the stairs two at a time. But when he pulled the door open, it wasn't Lia standing on the step. It was Eleonore, his mother.

Seth's face froze with shock. "Mother—is something wrong?"

"Are you going to invite me in?" she said tartly. "Or keep me waiting on the front step?"

"Sure…come in. I've got fresh coffee on, would you like some?"

"For heaven's sake, put some clothes on, Seth."

"I wasn't expecting you," he said dryly. "Make yourself at home, I'll be right down."

When he came back, Eleonore was sitting ramrod-straight in the living room in a very expensive chair made by a Finnish designer. She said irritably, "This chair is astonishingly comfortable—I can't imagine why."

He passed her a paper-thin porcelain cup of coffee. Eleonore took a sip and put the cup down on a leather-topped table. For once, she seemed to have nothing to say. Seth said casually, "You got my invitation to the wedding?"

"Yes. To the fiddle player. I thought you were against marriage."

"I am. Marise wants us to get married…so we are."

Looking out the window, Eleonore said stiffly, "Will your father be there?"

Seth nodded. "He and Marise hit it off right away."

"You know he's left me. He'll never forgive me. The child

all those years ago. And now keeping his grandchild a secret from him the last eight years."

"You could meet Marise, if you wanted to."

"I never thought he'd leave me!"

In the morning light coming through the tall windows, Seth could see his mother had aged in the last few weeks. Or was it simply that she'd lost some of her formidable self-control? "It came as a surprise to me, too," he said.

Eleonore bowed her head, twisting her fingers with their array of diamonds. "I—I miss him."

"He's changed," Seth said. "He'll never take orders from you again."

"I realize that, Seth," Eleonore snapped. "I'm not in my dotage yet."

"So what are you going to do about it?"

Eleonore fiddled with the diamond-studded bracelet of her watch. "I'm afraid to contact him. He might say he wants a divorce. That he's finished with me."

"He told me about your childhood, how—"

"He had no business telling you that!"

"Yes, he did," Seth said forcibly, "because it helped me understand you. You were never loved as a child—not as you should have been. You were beaten and abused instead. So you've been protecting yourself from love ever since. Refusing to give anyone else what you'd been so brutally denied."

But wasn't he speaking of himself? For years he'd been protecting himself in just the same way.

"Love's a trap," his mother retorted. "Let it in, and it destroys you."

"The lack of it is destroying you now," Seth said. "I can see it in your face."

Eleonore's mouth thinned. "How dare you talk to me that way."

But both of them had heard the quaver in her voice. "Phone

Dad," Seth said gently. "I don't think he's ever stopped loving you...why don't you see if I'm right?"

"If you're wrong, then I'll make a complete and utter fool of myself."

"If you don't get in touch with him, then you're a coward," Seth said grimly; and once again knew he was talking to himself.

"After I ran away from home, I swore I'd never be afraid of anyone again," Eleonore said haughtily.

Seth held out the portable phone. "Prove it to me."

"It would seem I've misjudged you, Seth—you've inherited more than your share of my pushiness."

"I believe you're right," Seth said, and punched in his father's number. After passing his mother the phone, he walked out of the room.

He had a phone call to make, too, he thought. To Lia. Although he had no idea what he was going to say.

He could start with *I'm sorry*. For hiding behind the past. For allowing it to dictate his life. For hurting her.

Five minutes later, Eleonore joined him in the kitchen, where he was gazing sightlessly into the garden. She said stiffly, "Your father and I are meeting in fifteen minutes on the steps of the Metropolitan Museum. We're going for a walk in Central Park, then he's taking me out for lunch."

"A date," Seth said naughtily.

She sniffed. "I guess I should thank you."

"I guess you should." He grinned, picked her up and whirled her around; she was lighter than he'd expected. "Have fun. Eat big globs of whipped cream. Don't forget to tell Dad you love him."

"Seth, put me down!"

She looked so scandalized, Seth started to laugh; and saw, to his great satisfaction, that Eleonore was smothering a smile. "Do you want me to call a cab?" he asked.

"I shall walk," Eleonore announced. "Years ago, your father used to give me a single yellow rose every month on the anniversary of our wedding. I might buy him one. On the way."

Seth kissed his mother on both cheeks. "I think that's a fine idea," he said thickly.

Staring at his shirtfront, she said rapidly, "I did a terrible thing—the abortion, I mean. But when I was a little girl my mother went through pregnancy after pregnancy, and each one dragged her further down...I should never have destroyed those letters, either. It was very wrong of me."

Her eyes were wet. Seth said huskily, "Sometimes tears can be more precious than apologies, Ma."

She looked him right in the eye. "I've wasted a great deal of my life, Seth. Don't do the same. I'd prefer to be called Mum, not Ma." Then she marched out the front door and down the steps.

Her advice was stunning in its simplicity.

All he had to do was take it.

CHAPTER FIFTEEN

As SETH went back inside, his cellphone started ringing. He took it out of his pocket, afraid it might be Allan saying he'd changed his mind.

"Seth?" Lia gasped. "Oh, Seth, is that you?"

His heart closed with terror. "What's wrong? Lia, what's the matter?"

"I'm in a terrible—just a minute."

He heard garbled voices in the background. Then she came back on. "I don't know—"

"Marise—has something happened to her? For God's sake, Lia, answer me."

"I would if you'd stop interrupting! Marise is fine, she's staying at Suzy's. Seth, I was so upset by the reviews that I left my violin on the back seat of a cab." Her voice wavered. "My priceless violin. My Strad."

In a great surge of relief that it was only a violin, Seth said, "Where are you?"

"I'm in another cab. Going to a pawnshop. That's where the first cab went after it let me off." Quickly she gave him the address.

"You're not to go there on your own—that's a really rough area of town. Stop the cab now, Lia, and I'll catch up with you."

"No way! I could never replace that violin, its tone is gor-

piness, her hair swirling in the wind. "I think they deserve an encore," she said, and launched into a fierce flamenco dance. As the elderly woman lifted her arms, clicking imaginary castanets, Seth began to dance with her.

Had he ever been as happy as he was right now?

The dance ended as wildly as it had begun. Seth bowed to the black-clad woman. Lia said breathlessly, once the applause had died down, "This gentleman had bought my violin from the pawnshop, for his daughter."

The little girl was gazing up at Seth with big, dark eyes that were very like Lia's. "We'll buy her another violin," Seth said.

"And I'll give her lessons," Lia promised.

"In the meantime, dearest Lia, I have a cab waiting to take you home," Seth said. "I wish it was a pure white steed."

She put her violin back in its case, gave the little girl's father her card and wrote down his phone number. Then, hand in hand, she and Seth started off down the sidewalk. Lacing her fingers with his, Lia said, "A cab is fine. A steed of any color would take longer."

"Are you in a hurry?" he said innocently.

"Yes," she said, "I want to go to bed with you."

Abruptly he turned to her, tracing the soft line of her lip with his fingertip. "I'm so sorry I caused you pain—I was so convinced I couldn't fall in love."

"Just as well," she teased, "at least it kept you from falling in love with anyone else."

"Maybe, deep down, I knew you were waiting for me."

"Oh Seth, we're going to be so happy!"

"I suspect my mother and my father will come to the wedding. Together. I'll warn her not to call you a fiddle player."

"If she does, she might find out that I'm more than her match. You've forgiven her, haven't you?"

"Forgiven her. Let go of that night in the library. Opened

my heart to the most beautiful woman in the world. It's been quite a morning."

Lia laughed. "Here's the ultimate test—Marise's idea of a flower girl seems to involve throwing daisies and snapdragons at all the guests. With Suzy egging her on. Can you handle that?"

"Sounds like fun. How about in the fall we host a very big party at the hotel in Paris where we met?".

"That sounds like fun, too."

"But first things first," he said firmly. "Bed."

The cabbie was still behind the wheel, snoring loudly. Seth took the opportunity to kiss Lia again. Then he tapped on the window, and they climbed in the back seat. Seth gave his address. "No rush this time," he said. "I found her. The woman I've been waiting for all my life."

"I should get an extra big tip for that," the cabbie drawled.

"You will," Seth said.

Twenty minutes later, the cabbie drove away looking very pleased with life. Seth unlocked his front door, then picked Lia up, violin and all, and carried her over the threshold. "Getting in practice," he grunted, locking the door behind him.

"So that's why you want to take me to bed—just to stay in practice?" she asked, wide-eyed.

"I'm taking you to bed because it feels like forever since I've had my arms around you. Because you're gorgeous and sexy and I love you to distraction."

She laughed, a cascade of pure delight. "I love you, too, darling Seth. And you know what they say—practice makes perfect."

Seth cupped her face in his palms, such a wealth of love in his eyes that Lia's heart melted in her breast. "You're perfect already," he said.

Introducing a brand-new miniseries

FOR *Love* OR MONEY

This is romance on the red carpet...

For Love or Money is the ultimate reading experience
for the reader who has a taste for tales of wealth and
celebrity and the accompanying gossip and scandal!

Look out for the special covers
and
these upcoming titles:

Coming in November:
SALE OR RETURN BRIDE
by Sarah Morgan

#2500

Coming in December:
TAKEN BY THE HIGHEST BIDDER
by Jane Porter

#2508

Harlequin Presents®
The ultimate emotional experience!

HARLEQUIN®
Presents

Seduction and Passion Guaranteed!

www.eHarlequin.com   HPSORB

If you enjoyed what you just read,
then we've got an offer you can't resist!

Take 2 bestselling
love stories FREE!
Plus get a FREE surprise gift!

geous. Indescribable. Plus it's worth a ton of money—I've got to find it."

His fiery Lia was back, in full force. "Give me the address of the pawn shop, I'll be there as soon as I can. Wait for me there—that's an order."

"Huh," she said, sounding slightly less upset. "It'll depend whether I get the violin back or not."

He was stuffing his wallet in his pants pocket and going out the door as he spoke. "My car's at the garage. I'll have to take a cab. Hell's teeth, Lia, don't put your life at risk—it's only a violin."

"Only?" she repeated incredulously.

"You're a thousand times more important to me than any violin—do you hear me? I can see a cab, I've got to go."

He flagged the cab down and tersely gave the address of the pawn shop. "An extra fifty bucks if you can get me there in fifteen minutes."

Settling back in the seat, Seth punched in Lia's number on his cell phone. An impersonal male voice said, "Your party is unavailable at this time. Please try again later."

Cursing under his breath, Seth jabbed the numbers again, only to get the same recording. She'd turned her cell phone off.

Or had someone done it for her, against her will? Had she run into trouble at the pawnshop?

As the cab whipped across two lanes of traffic, Seth was thrown sideways in the seat. Two words were drumming through his veins. Too late. Too late.

What if he was too late? What if something had happened to Lia?

He couldn't bear to lose her. His life would be meaningless without her.

Bathed in a cold sweat, he tried her number again. He could get to hate that guy's voice, he thought viciously, not as much as blinking as the cab squeezed between a garbage truck and a bus. Where was Lia? She had to be safe. She had to be.

In exactly thirteen minutes, the cabbie drew up outside a seamy little shop on an even seamier street. "You want me to wait?" he asked. "This don't look so great."

"Yeah…I'll be right out."

Seth ran for the door, which was weighted with heavy metal bars. He went inside and knew instantly that Lia wasn't there. He said to the proprietor, a man of indeterminate age who looked as though he'd been exposed to every vice humanity was capable of, "A woman was just here, looking for a violin. Where did she go?"

"What's it worth to you?"

"If I had more time, you and I could have a fascinating discussion on that subject." Seth banged his fist on the counter. "Tell me where she went."

"Okay, okay." The proprietor named a street in a nearby Puerto Rican neighborhood. "Some fella bought the violin. Real quick turnaround."

"If she's not there," Seth said pleasantly, "I'll be back. You'd better hope she's there."

The cab was still waiting. Seth gave the new address, bracing himself as they screeched around corners and edged through gaps that looked far too narrow. The vehicle jerked to a halt near the end of a street. "This is it," the cabbie said dubiously.

Seth got out. Over the racket from a construction site and the shrill voices of kids playing on the street, he heard, unmistakably, the sound of a violin. He said to the cabbie, thrusting some money through the window, "Another fifty if you'll wait."

"Sure thing." The cabbie leaned back, tipping his hat over his eyes.

Seth ran down the street. The passionate lilt of a Spanish dance echoed among the buildings, with their rusted fire escapes and cluttered sidewalks. He rounded a pizza joint, and saw Lia standing in front of a blue metal Dumpster, wearing a flowered skirt and a scoop-necked T-shirt, her beloved violin tucked under her chin. A small crowd surrounded her: men, women and children, stamping their feet, dancing and singing.

Briefly he sagged against the nearest wall, his breath rasping in his throat. She was safe. She hadn't been mugged, raped, murdered or kidnapped: any of the dreadful fates that imagination and terror had been conjuring up in his mind.

Who else but Lia would play her heart out on a windy street corner for people who probably couldn't afford even the cheapest of seats for one of her concerts?

Straightening, he walked toward her. She saw him coming, gave him a gamine grin and, with a grandiloquent flourish, finished the dance. The crowd burst into cheers and clapping.

When he reached her, she was still smiling. "Hi, Seth," she said. "I got my violin back."

"So you did." Holding her gaze, Seth got down on one knee on the grimy sidewalk. Her toenails were now painted a vibrant pink, to go with her fuchsia-colored shirt.

A fascinated silence fell, in which he heard, like faraway birds, the cries of the street children. He said formally, "Lia d'Angeli, I love you. *Te quiero. Te amo.* I've loved you ever since that night in Paris eight years ago. I love you with all my heart and all my soul. I loved you yesterday, I love you today, and I'll love you for all our tomorrows."

Lia had lowered her violin. She said blankly, "You're kidding."

"I've never been more serious in my life."

"Then you've lost it."

"Stop arguing—or I might change my mind."

"But you said you'd never fall in love."

"I was wrong, I was a fool. *Bufón. Idiota.* I came to my

senses this morning." His voice cracked. "Tell me I'm not too late. That you still love me and you'll marry me, be the bride of my heart."

A satisfied sigh emanated from the crowd. Lia was now blushing. "You've fallen in love with me—you're sure about that?"

He grinned, shifting his knee. "I'm as sure that I love you as this sidewalk's hard. Try not to keep me in suspense too long, huh?"

"You deserve to be kept in suspense," she said severely. "I've been very unhappy ever since I agreed to marry you."

He reached for her hand and raised it to his lips, kissing it with all the love in his heart. "I swear I'll do my utmost to make you happy every day of my life."

Her blush deepened. "What made you realize you loved me?"

"My mother came for a visit this morning. She was all shook up...different than I've ever seen her. She actually said she was sorry for what she'd done, she had tears in her eyes...and when she left, she was planning to buy my father a yellow rose. If she can do that, I can smash the barriers I've been hiding behind. I have smashed them. But then when you phoned, I thought something terrible had happened to you, and that I was too late. That I'd never be able to tell you I love you."

An elderly woman in a long black dress, a black headscarf over her hair, sighed softly, *"Te amo."* A young man put his arm around his heavily pregnant wife. Lia gave a sudden rich chuckle. "The audience is on your side, Seth."

"I need all the help I can get."

She pulled him to his feet. "I long to be your wife, *querido*. To be your beloved."

"Finally we've got it right," Seth said, kissing her passionately and at some length.

It was Lia who broke free. Her eyes were blazing with hap-

Coming Next Month

THE BEST HAS JUST GOTTEN BETTER!

#2499 THE DISOBEDIENT VIRGIN Sandra Marton
The Ramirez Brides

Catarina Mendes has been dictated to all her life. Now, with her twenty-first birthday, comes freedom—but it's freedom at a price. Jake Ramirez has become her guardian. He must find a man for her to marry. But Jake is so overwhelmed by her beauty that he is tempted to keep Cat for himself...

#2500 SALE OR RETURN BRIDE Sarah Morgan
For Love or Money

Sebastien Fiorukis is to marry Alesia Philipos. Their families have been feuding for generations, but it seems finally the rift is healed. However, all is not as it seems. Alesia has been bought by her husband—and she will *not* be a willing wife!

#2501 THE GREEK'S BOUGHT WIFE Helen Bianchin
Wedlocked!

Nic Leandros knows that people are only after his money. So when he finds that beautiful Tina Matheson is pregnant with his late brother's child, he's certain her price will be high. Tina must agree to his terms: they will marry for the baby's sake...

#2502 PREGNANCY OF REVENGE Jacqueline Baird
Bedded by Blackmail

Charlotte Summerville was a gold digger according to billionaire Jake d'Amato and he planned to take revenge in his bed! Suddenly innocent Charlie was married to a man who wanted her, but hated her...and she was pregnant with his child...

#2503 THE ITALIAN DOCTOR'S MISTRESS Catherine Spencer
International Doctors

Successful neurosurgeon Carlo Rossi has a passion for his work—and for women. And he desires Danielle Blake like no other woman. He insists they play by his rules—no future, just a brief affair. But when it's time for Danielle to leave Italy can he let her go?

#2504 BOUND BY BLACKMAIL Kate Walker
The Alcolar Family

Jake Taverner wants Mercedes Alcolar. So when she rejects him in the most painful way, his hurt pride demands revenge. Jake traps Mercedes into a fake engagement and embarks on a skillful seduction. But though he can bind her by blackmail...can he keep her?

HPCNM1005